Clara froze, her jaw

It was *him* from last night. Naked VIP Guy. And he was looking at her as if he'd expected their paths to cross.

Clara snatched her eyes away, fury and confusion knocking the air from her lungs.

"No pulse," he said, his gray-blue gaze landing on Clara's. "Are you okay to continue compressions, Nurse Lund?"

She nodded, tired but not yet spent.

Clara restarted the chest compressions, acutely aware that the man with the body of a Greek god and haunted eyes was now watching her every move while they tried to bring back Mr. Engman.

How dare he ambush her this way. How dare he be a doctor and not the diplomat she'd assumed.

How dare he be so calm and collected, as if he had no recollection of last night's knee-buckling kiss.

Only Clara's shame was amplified by how out of character she'd acted last night, how easily duped she'd been, flirting outrageously with and then kissing a sexy gloriously naked stranger who'd clearly deceived her about his true identity.

What had she been thinking?

Dear Reader,

In writing *Nurse's Secret Royal Fling*, I was totally swept along in the magic and sparkle of my hero's royal world and the mountainous principality of Varborg. Giving Prince Andreas Cronstedt such a grounded and cynical heroine in nurse Clara Lund led to lots of juicy tension, which was offset by their red-hot romance! I hope you enjoy reading about the medical emergencies that bring them together as well as the passionate love story that unfolds.

Love,

JC x

NURSE'S SECRET ROYAL FLING

JC HARROWAY

MEDICAL ROMANCE

Harlequin®
MEDICAL ROMANCE

Recycling programs for this product may not exist in your area.

ISBN-13: 978-1-335-59549-2

Nurse's Secret Royal Fling

Copyright © 2024 by JC Harroway

Harlequin Enterprises ULC
22 Adelaide St. West, 41st Floor
Toronto, Ontario M5H 4E3, Canada
www.Harlequin.com

Printed in U.S.A.

Lifelong romance addict **JC Harroway** took a break from her career as a junior doctor to raise a family and found her calling as a Harlequin author instead. She now lives in New Zealand and finds that writing feeds her very real obsession with happy endings and the endorphin rush they create. You can follow her at jcharroway.com and on Facebook, Twitter and Instagram.

Books by JC Harroway

Harlequin Medical Romance

A Sydney Central Reunion

Phoebe's Baby Bombshell

Gulf Harbour ER

Tempted by the Rebel Surgeon
Breaking the Single Mom's Rules

Forbidden Fling with Dr. Right
How to Resist the Single Dad
Her Secret Valentine's Baby

Visit the Author Profile page
at Harlequin.com for more titles.

To the wonderful and talented editors who helped
create this story. To Jo Grant, who believed that
Andreas and Clara's story deserved to be told,
and to Charlotte Ellis, who encouraged me
to take my characters on an emotion-packed journey
to their HEA.

CHAPTER ONE

CLARA LUND NEEDED this prestigious job. However *delicate* the situation awaiting her behind the intimidatingly vast timber door in the guest wing of Varborg's winter palace, she could handle it.

Straightening her crisply ironed nurse's uniform, she pressed the intercom button beside the door. Talk about being thrown in at the deep end on her first shift: no welcome tour of the palace; no explanation of her night-nurse duties; no pointers on royal protocol for when she finally did meet her patient, Prince Henrik, Varborg's ruler. When the intercom remained silent, Clara pressed the button again, for longer this time.

'Yes, yes. Please enter,' a disembodied male voice, deep and cultured, barked brusquely.

Rude... But at least he'd said 'please'.

The automatic locking system disarmed with a click. Clara pushed her way inside the suite and closed the door, focussed on her salary rather than the occupant's apparent sense of entitlement. It seemed, by working for Varborg's royal family, she'd have to get used to demanding VIPs. But this second salary would increase Clara's contribution to paying off the mortgage on her family's home and hopefully ease the perpetual worry lines around her mother's eyes.

Bypassing the ridiculously opulent fresh flower arrangement on the reception table, Clara set off in search of the grumpy-sounding guest. The suite boasted wall-to-wall luxury disguised beneath understated Scandinavian elegance. Were her feet not so deeply embedded in the concrete of reality, she might have spared a moment to be impressed.

Except each room was empty.

'Hello…?' she called out as she stepped into the deserted bedroom.

A splash of water sounded from the *en suite* bathroom.

'In here,' the owner of the rich baritone said from behind the half-open door.

'Are you okay, sir?' she asked, mostly keeping the exasperation from her voice. The guest sounded younger than she'd first assumed—and mildly irritated, as if she'd kept him waiting. 'I was led to believe that there was some sort of emergency.'

If his 'delicate situation' had been that urgent, someone would have called an ambulance.

The stranger sighed. 'The situation *is* urgent to me.'

'I did buzz. *Twice*,' she pointed out, his manner ruffling her usually unflappable feathers. He sounded perfectly healthy.

'I'm aware,' he said. 'Look, I'm sort of…stuck.'

Clara rolled her eyes. She wasn't a maid. An experienced nurse with her training—which included

a Master's degree in Advanced Clinical Practice—
was surely above reaching for the soap for some
entitled visiting dignitary or foreign ambassador?
Except patients, like customers, were always right.

Think about the money... Think about the money...

'I have no desire to waste your time,' he continued in that commanding voice she found both ob-
jectionable and inconveniently appealing. 'Could
you please enter so we can get this...*situation* over
with?'

'Okay—are you decent?' While she'd seen it all
before, she didn't want to barge in and embarrass
the owner of that attractive voice.

'I'm naked, if that's what you mean,' he replied,
his voice now tinged with amused challenge. 'But,
rest assured, I have no immediate plans to flash
you.'

Clara stifled a snigger. A sense of humour helped
when patients were forced to concede their dignity
and ask for assistance.

'That's good,' she quipped, pressing her lips together to contain her smile. 'We don't want a sexual harassment incident on my first night, do we?'

When her only reply was a dry chuckle that filled
her belly with inexplicable flutters of excitement,
Clara pushed the door fully open and poked her
head inside.

Any trace of humour drained from her like water
down a gold-plated plughole. There was nothing
laughable about the modern-day Viking reclining
regally in the generous bath, which looked as if it

could happily accommodate two adults with ample room for fun and games.

Clara's mouth instantly turned dry, her pulse speeding as he arched one golden brow, his bold blue-grey stare defiant and full of questions.

'Um…hello,' she croaked, stepping from behind the door.

To her utter alarm, her face warmed. Every spirited retort deserted her, while the shocking heat of instant attraction set her entire body aflame, as if she'd rolled naked in a bed of nettles.

'You're a nurse,' he said with surprise, a frown slashing his outrageously handsome face as he looked her up and down.

Her body heated in every place his eyes landed. How could he do that? And was it her imagination, or was he vaguely familiar? She rarely watched TV, was too busy for social media and had no time for VIP-spotting.

'Well observed,' she said dryly, looking away. Not because he was naked, concealed only from the waist down by what she suspected was a dwindling foam of bubbles, but because, trapped or not, he dominated the luxurious marble bathroom like some sort of powerfully virile mountain-man.

She exhaled slowly, grateful for that modesty layer of suds. His voice alone was sexy in a bossy kind of way, but the entire package seemed to have triggered a rush of hormones—no mean feat considering that Clara deliberately avoided noticing members of the opposite sex. Relationships weren't worth her while. Even sex, the one time she'd done it, had been underwhelming, leaving her vulnerable and humiliated.

But she'd have to be anaesthetised not to notice *this* man.

'The east wing steward sent me,' she said, casually scanning the room for signs of blood or trauma, while she willed her body to revert to normal. 'But I'll happily leave again if you were expecting someone else. A plumber, perhaps…?'

He laughed, another dry chuckle that rumbled up from that deliciously broad chest. She couldn't remember the last time someone had found her funny or made her laugh in return. Absurdly, Clara searched for other amusing things to say.

Except this was work. She was a professional. She wasn't here to spar with him, no matter how carefree and giggly he made her feel.

'*Are* you hurt?' she asked sharply, pointedly glancing at the watch pinned to her pocket before scrutinising his well-defined chest, which was covered in manly hair with the barest hint of reddish gold. His shoulders were wide, his upper body ripped and bronzed. While she desperately tried not to envision herself as the second occupant of that giant bath, Clara's gaze skimmed the ladder of his abs until she reached the modesty layer of suds, frustrated to have her view cruelly interrupted.

'Don't mind me,' he drawled, snapping her to her senses. 'Have a good, long look.' He relaxed his arms on the edge of the bath as if in invitation.

'As you pointed out,' she blustered, mortified to be caught ogling the sexy, naked VIP, 'I'm a medical professional—I was assessing you for injuries.'

'Is that right?' He raised his eyebrows, a knowing smile tugging at one corner of his sensual mouth, which was surrounded by a close-cropped beard of dark facial hair flecked with similar golden tones to his body hair.

'Indeed.' Clara tilted her chin, hot shame in her veins that she'd temporarily forgotten she was there to help him; that it was her *job*, one she couldn't afford to mess up. 'And I'm pleased to find that you seem fine.'

If 'fine' denoted the kind of wildly rugged male beauty that brought to mind log cabins in the snowy mountains, fur pelts on the floor, a crackling fire…

Where the hell had that ridiculous and unwarranted fantasy come from? His raw, edgy sex appeal was as irrelevant as his VIP status. She wasn't about to undo the past eight years of struggle and heartache for something as frivolous as sexual chemistry.

From the age of sixteen, when her father had left his wife and two daughters and done a runner, Clara, the eldest, had worked part-time to contribute to the family income. At nineteen, while Clara had also been studying for her nursing degree, her mother, Alma, had developed breast cancer and hadn't been able to work for months on end while undergoing treatment. Clara's income had kept the roof over their heads and the bills paid with no help from her absent father. The emotional toll of caring for Alma, while also taking on financial responsibility for her family, had cured teenaged Clara of the foolish romantic aspirations of most of her peers.

Especially after Alma discovered her father, Lars, had re-mortgaged the house to fund one of his get-rich-quick schemes and had then ended up in prison for fraud. Now, at twenty-four, with her parents' unequal marriage as a warning, Clara's only goal was lifelong financial and emotional independence. She'd never be *any* man's puppet, wild mountain-men and Vikings included.

'I need to get back to work,' she said in her haughtiest voice, willing her eyes to steer clear of his ripped physique. 'So unless you're bleeding to death...'

She paused expectantly, faking indifference to the inconvenient attraction that, for a moment, had caught her off-guard.

'No blood. Sorry to disappoint you.' His lips twitched with playful amusement other women might have found charming.

No doubt he was used to the effect he had on poor unsuspecting women. Only, Clara had seen how love could make one partner, usually the woman, vulnerable. Her mother had excused and forgiven Lars time and time again in the name of love.

Ignoring the heat and speculation in his stare, she smiled sweetly. 'What a shame.'

'Next time, I'll try to provide you with a little

more drama,' he said, his silvery blue eyes sparkling flirtatiously.

'Let's hope there'll be no next time,' she shot back, unable to resist. Was this the flirty fun she'd missed out on as a teenager because of Lars's irresponsible approach to raising his daughters?

At that he only stared, amused and revoltingly confident in his nudity.

'So, what can I do for you?' She folded her arms across her chest, keeping her eyes on his face and not a millimetre lower. Now that he seemed to have awoken a previously dormant aspect of her womanhood, all she could think about was escape. *He* was the naked one, but she felt horribly exposed, imagining wildly romantic scenarios when, before meeting him, she'd have sworn that there wasn't a fanciful bone in her body.

'While that's normally the kind of offer I'd love to hear from a beautiful woman,' he said, his stare playfully daring, 'We've already vetoed sexual harassment, although you might need to stop looking at me as if you've been denied the last cookie in the jar.'

His comment drew another uncontrollable blush from Clara. A trickle of fear chilled her blood as if by ignoring the demands of her femininity up to now something vital might be missing from her life and somehow he could tell.

'You said you were stuck. And I'm not interested in cookies,' she lied, dragging her eyes away from his chest.

How had they got there again? Was he some sort of sickeningly handsome sorcerer, bewitching her with his hot bod, his sparkly eyes and the sheer force of his unapologetic masculinity?

'In that case,' he said, seeming to drop the cocky attitude, 'I won't keep you from your other duties any longer.'

'How generous,' she snapped, the testosterone fog around him the only excuse for her uncharacteristic attitude. 'I'd hate to have to attend to a *real* emergency and leave you…indisposed. I'm sure that bath is getting cold.'

She just couldn't seem to bite her tongue around him.

He laughed, something like respect flickering in his eyes. Validation shot excitement along Clara's nerves, lighting her up inside like the million stars in the night sky. She fisted her hands on her hips, furious at her rebellious body's response to him. If circumstances had been different, if they'd been equals, if she hadn't needed this lucrative job, she would have turned tail and left him to shiver in his cooling bathwater.

Instead, she clamped her lips together. Her family was one defaulted mortgage repayment away from losing their home.

As if finally done toying with her, the infuriating man sat up. The water swirled around his lean hips in tantalisingly hypnotic currents.

'Before you leave,' he said, the amused lilt lingering in his voice telling her he'd caught her watching those currents for a glimpse of what lay beneath. 'I wonder if you would save me an undignified crawl across the tiles and be so kind as to pass me my leg?'

CHAPTER TWO

CROWN PRINCE ANDREAS CRONSTEDT, heir to the Varborg throne, was rarely surprised by the many people he met. But the enchanting beauty who'd marched into his bathroom with her no-nonsense attitude didn't bat an eyelid at his rather unusual request.

'Of course,' she said, casting big, blue eyes around the bathroom. 'Your leg; where might I find that?'

Satisfaction spread through the ancient Viking blood in Andreas's veins like lava. She was spectacular. And obviously had no idea that he descended from a long, ancient line of Scandinavian princes.

'Try behind you, in the bedroom. Under the curtains, perhaps?' Andreas indicated the doorway, through which this fascinating and forthright woman had come. 'I'm quite impressed with myself for making such an improbable shot.'

'What is it doing all the way over there, when you're stuck in your *cold* bath?' she asked, casting him an unsympathetic look he found thrilling.

Rather than having the desired effect, her taunting reprimand, and the way she looked at him with both interest and astonishment at his stupidity, flooded his groin with heat. Too bad she was a palace employee, one of the round-the-clock nurses employed to keep Prince Henrik in excellent health, and therefore strictly off-limits.

'I'm afraid I hurled it away, unthinkingly, in a rare fit of frustration,' he said, gleefully admitting to this intriguing stranger that his current predicament was totally self-inflicted.

'So you only have yourself to blame,' she pointed out, one hand on her hip.

Had anyone ever before found him ridiculous? Had a woman ever stirred his curiosity so...intensely? Right then he couldn't recall a single time.

'I'm afraid so.' He smiled, noticing how her lips twitched, as if she was trying not to laugh.

'Interesting...' she said and turned away.

As Prince Henrik's second, less important son, Andreas had been allowed to pursue a career of his choosing. As a doctor, he met a lot of nurses, but none as unique, strikingly beautiful or unapologetically herself as this one. Where on Earth had the palace found such a refreshingly candid character?

Through the open door, he watched her stoop in search of his leg. As she looked behind the heavy curtains, Andreas willed his eager anatomy into submission. But he was only a man, not superhuman. He couldn't have stopped his stare sliding to the curve of her hips and derrière as she bent over if his life had depended upon it. Perhaps he should turn on the cold tap, shock his libido into behaving, but where was the fun in that?

And tonight, after having been rudely summoned home, his locum position in Stockholm cut short by his father's personal secretary with only the briefest of explanations—Prince Henrik was fatigued following a short illness and needed time to recover—Andreas deserved a little flirtatious interlude with a woman for whom he was just an ordinary man.

Excitement buzzed through his nervous system at the heady freedom this encounter offered. Most people recognised Varborg's physically challenged prince, a man who was not meant to rule and could never replace his late older brother, the popular Oscar. But, with *this* woman, he had the opportunity for complete anonymity; to be no one but himself for a moment.

He'd never met anyone like her, least of all in his royal life, in which women were cookie-cutter sophisticates who fitted into two categories: those who fawned and flattered him and those too intimidated by his title to utter a single word. Even the women he bedded were careful to avoid any verbal display beyond voicing their delight between the sheets, should it somehow lose them his royal favour.

On discovering he was an amputee, some went overboard on the sympathy, infantilised him. He might have lost a leg, but the rest of him worked just fine, as proved by the very functional stirring in his groin that this delightful stranger had provoked the minute she peered into the room with her cutting remarks and her prim and proper hairdo.

'Found it,' she said, returning to the bathroom, flushed and slightly breathless in a way that made him think of kissing. 'Luckily for you.'

He was lucky that she'd been the one sent to his aid. If he'd known that *she* awaited him, he might not have been so reluctant to return to the oppressive confines of the palace, all be it to the guest wing he'd insisted upon. He wasn't ready to sleep in the suite that had once belonged to Oscar. Nor did he intend to be solely at the crown's beck and call just because he'd returned to help out Prince Henrik with royal engagements. He'd taken a locum position at the local private medical clinic, his work the one thing in his life that filled him with uncomplicated pride.

'Thank you,' he said, savouring her striking face, her hair the colour of burnt caramel and the playful glint in her blue eyes. 'What's your name?'

He swept his gaze from her exquisite features down the length of her body, tracing her blistering figure underneath the nurse's uniform, in the way she'd blatantly appraised him earlier. 'I should have asked before, given the circumstances.'

'Circumstances,' she scoffed, holding out the prosthesis. 'Is that what we're calling a fit of leg-hurling impatience? I thought it was a self-inflicted situation.'

He grinned, waiting patiently for her answer, while her stare once more dipped to his torso in obvious admiration. She couldn't seem to stop checking him out.

When he made no move to take the leg, she huffed. 'My name is Clara. Clara Lund.'

A small smile tugged at his mouth—captivating, candid Clara. 'Pleased to meet you, Clara.'

Her name caressed his tongue the way he imagined her kiss would taste: breathy, bold, undaunted: like the woman herself. A woman who clearly didn't care one jot that he was someone important enough to stay at one of the Cronstedt palaces.

She frowned and shuddered a little, as if his speaking her name gave her a thrill of pleasure that was inconvenient. He understood her dilemma. Regardless of the sparks between them, he couldn't bed this woman whom the universe had delivered as if to soothe his grieving soul. Because being back home resurfaced complex emotions.

'Thank you for finding it.' He took the prosthesis, noting with satisfaction the way her eyes were averted from the layer of thinning suds that, just about, still concealed his lower half. 'You should know that not many people surprise me, Clara.'

'Well, I'm glad I could save you that undignified crawl across the tiles.'

Andreas's smile widened. The more they talked, the better he felt about being here, a place of bittersweet memories. She'd helped him forget that, one day, be it in five years or fifteen, he would have to abandon the medical career he loved and succeed his father. It wouldn't matter that, as the spare who'd been left to his own devices, he was unqualified for the role. Nor would it matter that the nation, who still referred to Andreas as 'the party prince' he'd been in his twenties, had adored Oscar, just like Prince Henrik—just like Andreas himself, in fact. He would have no choice but to turn his back on the life he'd built for himself and step into his brother's shoes.

'I'll be going, then, if that's everything...?' She glanced at the door, as if she was dying to escape.

He should let her go, but not yet.

'Yes, time to get out, I think.' Andreas propped his prosthesis against the side of the bath and pulled the plug. He braced his hands on the bath's edge as if to lever his body from the water, unable to resist one final flirtation, if only to see the censure once more sparking in her pretty eyes.

Right on cue, she flushed. 'Right... I'll...um... leave you to it.'

She cast one last look down his chest to the waterline and scurried from the room.

'I'd appreciate it if you could wait,' he called after her, a rumble of amusement trapped in his throat. 'I'd like to thank you properly—face to face, as it were. When I'm no longer naked.'

He heard a nervous squawk from the bedroom, neither a refusal nor acceptance, but some instinct told him that she'd wait.

Andreas used his upper-body strength to haul himself from the bath. He reached for a towel, impatient now to know everything there was to know about the palace's newest nurse, perhaps the only woman on the planet who'd failed to recognise him; a woman with whom he would be free simply to be an ordinary man—not Andreas, the second-choice heir.

He attached his below-knee prosthesis to his left leg and wrapped a fresh towel around his waist, swallowing down the sour taste of failure that being back here had caused to resurface. Judgement seemed to seep from the ancient palace walls. He wasn't meant to have been the one. It should have been Oscar in line to the throne.

If only Andreas had been able to save him. The defeat and guilt brought jarring flashes of his worst memory—a crumpled vehicle wreck, the smell of hot metal and petrol, the urgency to save his unconscious brother and his attempts at CPR. And then nothing but blackness until he'd woken up in hospital.

Why hadn't he died in that accident instead of Oscar? With the ruler who'd trained for the role from birth, the future of Varborg would have been secure. Whereas Andreas knew more about the human body than being a statesman.

He found Clara in the suite's living room, her back to the fire while she looked out at the shadowy, mountainous view beyond the windows. He clung to the distracting sight of her wonderful ordinariness. It made him want to be an ordinary man, not a last-resort prince. To shrug off the sense of being second best and feel invincible, the way he had when she'd moved her eyes over his nakedness. To be himself, the man she'd seen when she'd challenged him so unflinchingly.

'Beautiful, isn't it?' he said, entranced by the angles of her profile as he flicked on the lamps.

Clara turned to face him and gaped. Her throat moved on a pained-looking swallow that fanned his ego. 'You're still naked.' Her gobsmacked stare travelled down his bare torso, which was dotted with the droplets of water he'd missed in his haste to prolong their thrilling interaction.

'Not quite.' He shrugged, unabashed. 'Would you like a drink?' He poured himself a nightcap.

'No, thank you. I'm *supposed* to be working.' She fidgeted with her hair, pushing some unruly strands of honeyed gold behind her ear, while she tried valiantly to keep her eyes averted from his bare chest and the towel slung low on his hips.

Oh, yes, she felt this primal attraction as strongly as him, and the intense chemistry neither of them could dismiss, no matter how inconvenient or ill-judged.

'Well, I need to warm up after that tepid bath.' He joined her before the fire.

Something about her made him feel less alone, as if the ferocity of their attraction proved they were humans first, all other expectations second.

'You could always put some clothes on,' she snapped.

'I could.' Grateful to have their playful banter back, he made no move to oblige her. 'But then I'd miss the way you're looking at me.'

'I'm not looking at you. I'm wondering how soon I can return to my proper job.'

'Point taken. But, before you leave, tell me, do you work here full-time?' he asked, already looking forward to their next meeting.

'*Part*-time,' she stressed. 'I have another full-time job at a local hospital.'

'You work *two* jobs?' he asked, astonished by her impressive dedication.

'Some people must if they want a roof over their heads.' She cast him another of those challenging looks and then glanced around the immaculately elegant room, a barely concealed sneer on her lips.

Of course; the palace was completely over the top compared to how most normal people lived.

'Forgive me.' Andreas frowned, appalled by the arrogant assumptions he'd made about this intriguing woman's life. 'I've detained you long enough.'

But now he wanted to know everything about Clara Lund. To understand what had shaped her, what drove her, what dreams she held. Meeting her tonight had been a welcome-home gift he could never have anticipated. Knowing she worked in a place where he should feel at ease to be himself but instead felt like an imposter gave him the strength to face all that this place represented: memories, good and bad; expectations of duty and obligation at odds with his dreams; the disappointment in people's eyes, his father's included.

He placed his barely touched Scotch on the table and held out his hand, wishing he didn't have to let her go. 'It was a pleasure to meet you, Clara. Thank you for your help.'

She took his hand, her grip firm and her fingers warm, her touch calling to that part of him that was, first and foremost, a man.

'Perhaps you'll be more careful where you throw your prosthesis in future,' she said, those big, intelligent eyes teasing.

What did she see when she looked at him? Suddenly, he wanted to know.

'You haven't asked—about how I lost my leg.' He kept hold of her hand, hoping she couldn't feel the rapid acceleration of his pulse. 'Most people can't help their curiosity.'

But he'd already established this woman wasn't most people.

If she *did* ask, he'd have to confess his true identity, explain the accident and voice his worst failing to this extraordinary, ordinary woman. Would she view him differently if she knew how he'd failed his brother, his family, his nation? Would she too find him somehow lacking?

Could he stand to find out?

Her stare clung to his. 'If you wanted me to know, a complete stranger, you'd have told me.'

Andreas's breath caught in his chest, her answer more perfect than he could ever have imagined.

'And why does it matter?' she asked, her pupils dilating in the dim lighting. 'Our scars don't define us, do they?'

Her astonishing reply sliced through him like a blade. She couldn't possibly know he struggled with imposter syndrome, not because he'd lost a limb, but because he'd been raised from birth to know that he wasn't quite as important as his older brother, a brother who had then died on Andreas's watch.

'No, I suppose they don't,' he said, as fresh heat boiled inside him.

What scars had shaped beguiling, hard-working and independent Clara?

For Andreas, his injury represented what might have been, what *should* have been, if Oscar had survived the accident instead. His scars were a daily reminder of the brother he'd failed to save. And more—with Oscar dead, and his father growing older, Andreas would one day need to forgo his career and his freedom.

But she was right: there *was* more to him than his scars, his past mistakes and the future role he would one day inherit. In that moment, he was desperate to be nothing more than an ordinary man.

'May I?' he asked, slowly lifting his hand to an escaped lock of hair on her cheek.

She nodded, her eyes dipping to his mouth for a revealing second as her breathing accelerated.

This close, he could see a tiny hole in her nose from a piercing. It made him smile and strengthened his resolve to stand up to the palace's demands for his time, to cling to the medical career he loved, until he was finally forced to stop. He tucked the silky strand behind her ear, his fingers lingering over that soft golden hair.

Oh, Clara, Clara, Clara... Why is it so hard to let you walk away?

As if she'd read his mind, she gripped his wrist, holding his hand in place.

His pulse spiked. He should tell her to leave. Except her warm, feminine scent lured him as she swayed closer and wet her lips with the tip of her tongue, her hungry stare latched to his, as if she saw deep inside his soul.

'You should go,' he said in one last ditch attempt to do the right thing, to resist the madness engulfing him like a rogue wave sucking him under.

'I should.' She nodded, swallowed and inched closer.

Damn it, just one taste.

Crushing her to his bare chest, he covered her mouth with his, pressing her pliant body close, from breasts to hips. Need roared through his blood, powerful and inescapable, setting off a chain reaction of desire so intense, he lost his mind. Her lips were soft, her whimper a moan of desperation that echoed so deeply inside him he struggled to recall if he'd ever wanted a woman more.

She parted her lips and touched her tongue to his, twisting his hair in her greedy hands. He tasted sweet triumph. He wasn't alone. She felt this uncontrollable chemistry too.

Her body writhed against his as their kiss deepened. His towel loosened and slid from his hips to the floor. But he was too far gone to care, too intent on the thrilling duel of tongue against tongue, too aroused by the intense flare of mutual passion as they kissed.

With a sudden gasp, she broke free. She pushed at him, so he stepped back, releasing her at once.

Her hand flew to cover her mouth, but not before Andreas saw the evidence of her kiss-swollen lips. 'I'm sorry. I shouldn't have done that.' She looked down at his nakedness—he was hard—and stepped back towards the exit. 'You're a guest here.'

'No, I'm…here on business.' He speared his fingers through his hair, lingering arousal and fresh guilt shredding his composure. '*I'm* the one who's sorry. It was my fault.'

'Please don't have me fired,' she whispered, backing further away as if he was some sort of lecherous creep. 'I need this job.'

Fired? Guilt rattled his bones. 'There's no question that you'll lose your job.'

He'd taken advantage of the situation, kept his identity secret and indulged himself with a beautiful woman in his father's employment. Yes, she'd kissed him back, her passion as desperate as his, but he should have controlled himself. He knew better and held himself to higher standards than other men.

'Wait,' he said, reaching for his towel as she turned and headed for the exit.

He strode after her, tucking his towel around his waist. For a wild and irresponsible moment, he'd relished the freedom to be the anonymous man Clara saw, flirted with and found attractive. He would make this right and tell her his name, hope she didn't curtsey or something equally hideous, and perhaps they could laugh about the situation.

Except, by the time he reached the corridor, she'd disappeared. Andreas cursed under his breath. He closed the suite door and retraced his footsteps. The room seemed to have shrunk, the walls pressing in on him with the heavy weight of regret. He touched his lips, the lingering taste of Clara soured by the bitter taste of what might have been if he were any other man.

CHAPTER THREE

IF CLARA HAD hoped for a quiet moment the following day to analyse why she'd acted so completely out of character, flirting with and then kissing a gloriously naked stranger, she was to be sorely disappointed. No sooner had she met her newest patient at Nordic Care, a private hospital an hour's drive from the palace, than the poor elderly man collapsed and went into cardiac arrest right before her eyes.

Shocked into action, Clara hit the alarm on the wall above the patient's bed and instantly began chest compressions. The crash team arrived within seconds—two other nurses and a female registrar. The doctor began manually bagging the patient, inflating his lungs with air, while Clara gave the team a brief synopsis of the patient's medical problems.

'This is Mr Engman, a seventy-three-year-old diabetic admitted overnight with dizzy spells.'

Clara snatched a breath, the exertion of performing CPR talking all her energy. 'We'd been monitoring him for cardiac arrhythmias. I'd just taken over his care when he collapsed and lost consciousness.'

She didn't want to tell the doctor her job, but the heart monitor seemed to show ventricular fibrillation, an abnormal rhythm where the heart's ventricles quivered in an irregular and uncoordinated manner. Other staff arrived, bodies jostling in the cramped space around the bed. Emergencies like this prompted a kind of controlled, co-ordinated chaos that ensured there were enough hands on board to do everything they could to revive their patient.

Clara focussed on timing the cardiac compressions, willing Mr Engman to respond. But her stomach tightened with fear, given his frail condition and multiple comorbidities.

'Looks like ventricular fibrillation,' a male voice said from behind Clara, confirming her diagnosis.

She was too focussed on the CPR to wonder where she'd heard the vaguely familiar voice before.

'Check for a pulse, please,' the commanding voice ordered.

There was a pause while they checked if Mr Engman's heart had spontaneously restarted. Clara caught her breath, looking up at the man running the arrest protocol.

She froze, her jaw dropping.

It was *him*—from last night—the naked VIP. The man with the body of a Greek god and haunted eyes. And he was looking at her without a trace of surprise, as if he'd expected their paths to cross.

Last night, after they'd kissed as if competing for the Olympic gold medal in kissing, Clara had met others from the team of palace nursing staff who cared for Prince Henrik, praying she'd never need to see her sexy but confusing stranger again.

Except there he was—a sexy mountain-man in scrubs.

Clara snatched her gaze away from his, fury and humiliation turning her stomach. While she'd been high from the kiss and begging for her job, he'd secretively held on to some pretty pertinent information. So this was the *business* he'd vaguely referred to. He was a *doctor*. Why hadn't he just come out and said that last night? She'd assumed he was a diplomat or a visiting ambassador, and he'd said nothing to the contrary. He'd commented on her uniform but had failed to declare that they worked in the same field. She'd even told him she had a second job at a nearby hospital, just before he'd lured her with his vulnerable stare and his talk of scars into that disastrous kiss which might have cost her a lucrative and prestigious job at the palace.

'No pulse,' Naked VIP said. 'Are you okay to continue compressions, Nurse Lund?'

Mortified that she'd lusted after and kissed someone so apparently shifty, Clara nodded and restarted the chest compressions. This was why she couldn't trust men. The last time she'd been intimate with a guy, he'd slept with her and then avoided her. Ever since, she'd resolutely refused to give anyone the power to hurt and humiliate her. Until last night...

She should have known better. After all, she'd learned to rely only on herself after her father, the one man who should have offered unconditional emotional and financial support, had repeatedly let her down. Growing up, she'd never known from one day to the next if Lars would come through the door at the end of the day, if the bills she knew worried her hard-working mother would be paid or if her father's latest dodgy deal would topple, plunging the entire family into a deeper pit of debt and despair.

One of Clara's nurse colleagues stuck gel pads to Mr Engman's chest and Naked VIP—she really needed to discover his name—positioned the defibrillator paddles in place.

'Stand clear. Defibrillating—two hundred joules,' he said, delivering the shock to the man's failing heart in line with the Advanced Cardiac Life Support protocol.

Clara couldn't bear to look at him. He looked far too gorgeous in the hospital's navy-blue scrubs, and being lured by his irrelevant good looks was how she'd found herself in this embarrassing situation in the first place.

'Nothing,' her stranger said, watching the erratic trace on the cardiac monitor.

'It's been three minutes,' Clara told him, resuming the chest compressions, glad to have an excuse to look away from his annoyingly riveting lips.

He nodded, taking a vial of adrenaline from the trolley and administering it intravenously in an attempt to normalise the heart's rhythm.

Why had she kissed him? She'd allowed him to get under her skin, weakened by desire stronger than anything she'd ever known. Flirting with him had felt carefree, whereas growing up with her unreliable father and having to care for her mother had given Clara an over-inflated sense of responsibility. They'd talked about scars and he'd seemed momentarily lost, a feeling she'd understood well as a bewildered teenager.

Until that unexpected interlude in the palace's guest suite, she hadn't realised that Lars Lund's selfish actions meant that she'd missed out on a wild and misspent youth. But with *him*, a sexy, naked stranger, she'd felt young and vibrantly alive.

She'd have to stop thinking of him naked. It was foolish to think about him in any state given that he was just another man she couldn't trust.

'Pause please,' the man in question said. All eyes settled on the heart monitor, every member of staff awaiting Naked VIP's next instruction with bated breath.

'He's still in VF,' he said. 'Stand clear—defibrillating again.'

With the second shock delivered, Mr Engman's heart stuttered back into sinus rhythm, the patient breathing again of his own accord. There was a collective sigh of relief. Clara sagged, her head woozy from the physical exertion and the adrenaline rush.

'Okay, we'll be moving Mr Engman around to ICU,' her midnight mystery man said. 'Nurse Lund, can you please call Mr Engman's next of kin?'

'Of course.' Clara nodded and placed a high-flow oxygen mask on their still groggy patient. This necessitated stepping closer to *Dr* Naked VIP.

Big mistake. He smelled delicious, reminding her

of how it had felt to be held in those strong arms last night: safe, protected, desired.

The wild desperation of that kiss—his big body engulfing hers, each of their lips chasing the other's, demanding and sensual—had surely ruined her for all future kisses. For a second, before she'd pushed him away, Clara hadn't been able to come up with a single reason she shouldn't sleep with him right there and then.

Swallowing hard, Clara fought off visions of him naked and proud, a spectacular specimen of manhood. The magnificence of his manhood was of no consequence whatsoever. And, more importantly, Clara wasn't interested in kissing, naked or otherwise. His deception made her realise just how out of her depth she was when it came to relationships.

She reattached an electrode that had come loose during CPR to Mr Engman's chest. The mystery doctor drew some blood from the patient's arm, thrusting the vials at the registrar.

'Check his cardiac enzymes and do an ECG, please. We need to exclude a myocardial infarction or cardiomyopathy.'

'I can do the ECG, if you want,' Clara said to the harassed-looking registrar, who gave a grateful nod and hurried away to order the blood work, leaving Clara alone with the patient and *him*.

An awkward silence descended.

Clara felt his observation like sun on her face as she tucked in the blanket on Mr Engman's bed. The patient was obliviously out of it, but this wasn't the time or the place for a personal conversation.

She looked up, their stares locking. 'Any other tests you'd like, *doctor*?'

She emphasised his title, showing him, and more importantly herself, that whatever had happened during last night's moment of insanity wouldn't be happening again. She couldn't trust one glorious hair on his devious head.

An image of Alma Lund, weary, sick and scared, flashed behind her eyes. Her mother had been through so much, and had always worked hard to provide a stable and comfortable home for Clara and her younger sister Freja, latterly with no help from her husband.

Clara wanted to slap herself; she knew better than to risk anything for a man, especially the income that kept them in their family home.

'No thank you, Nurse Lund.' Curiosity flickered over his expression, his blue eyes impressed and carrying the same hint of vulnerability that, last night, had made her lose her mind.

Well, in the cold light of day, her head was back in charge. She didn't need his admiration. She didn't need to know his name. She didn't need him at all, not even for phenomenal naked kissing. What she needed were her two jobs, her peace of mind and her self-reliance.

'We need to talk,' he said, pausing at the gap in the curtains around Mr Engman's bed.

'Didn't we have that opportunity last night?' she

shot back, feeling decidedly uncharitable, given that she'd allowed herself to be duped by a charming smile, some witty repartee and a hot body.

'Last night, I was…distracted,' he admitted, pressing his lips together grimly as he continued to stare.

And just like that Clara's body returned to the scene of the crime—her pulse going crazy, her blood so hot she must surely have given off steam and the taste of him fresh on her lips.

A wave of fear and foolishness whipped through her chest. Even now—with every reason in the world not to; when last night's rash and unprecedented impulse to kiss a fellow lost soul might have cost her the job at the palace; when he held all of the power—she craved another kiss.

'Well, today I have my head screwed on correctly,' she said, willing it to be true.

It was only when he'd finally exited the ward moments later that Clara could finally breathe easy. Whatever he had to say, whatever his real name and his reasons for being secretive, he was just another man showing her the only person she could truly rely on was herself.

CHAPTER FOUR

LATER THAT MORNING, Andreas waited outside the acute medical ward for Clara Lund to emerge. She pushed through the doors and headed for the lifts, an assault to every one of his heightened senses. Today's uniform was navy, the fitted cut reminding Andreas how it had felt to have that insanely gorgeous body pressed against him last night while their tongues had duelled for dominance of their kiss.

He approached, his heart knocking at his ribs at the sight of her hair pulled back into a tight bun, leaving her slender neck exposed. Heaven help him; even now, when he had a whole heap of explaining to do, he wanted to remove the clips and tunnel his hands in all of that silkiness as he kissed her again and again until her eyes glazed with arousal once more.

'Clara,' he said, intercepting her outside the lift. 'Is now a good time to talk?'

If she remained ignorant of his identity after their reunion over this morning's crash call, it was time he filled in the blanks.

She glanced up, her expression carefully neutral. 'I'm on my lunch break, doctor.'

Her voice was deservedly dismissive; he missed

her playfulness. 'I appreciate that,' he said, regretting that he hadn't warned her about them working at the same hospital the moment he'd discovered the fact from palace security last night after she'd left. 'But what I have to say won't take long. I'll accompany you to the canteen. It will give me a chance to explain a few things.'

'Like how you're a doctor, not a diplomat?' Suspicion narrowed her eyes. 'I've already figured that out all by myself, thanks. The scrubs and white coat kind of give it away.'

She jabbed at the already lit up call button, as if desperate to escape.

Andreas winced with remorse but he was so glad to see her feisty side. Her anger was better than her indifference.

'It's…complicated,' he said, wishing he'd explained himself last night, in private.

Technically a prince *was* a diplomat, a representative of the nation he served.

'I'm kind of both, for the time being,' he added, frustrated by the thought that, given its way, Prince Henrik's office would have him abandon his career now and commit fully to royal duties. If he capitulated to the palace's demands, he would have to give up treating patients, give up his freedom to flirt with fascinating women like Clara and give up everything he'd known his entire adult life.

A dull throb of resentment tightened his chest. He loved his job and had worked hard for his career. He was good at being a doctor. Being back in

Varborg meant readjusting to the demands of his two personas: Andreas the man, free to do what he liked, and Andreas the prince.

'Great,' she scoffed, shaking her head with disbelief. 'That's cleared everything up.'

Andreas smiled to himself, his spirits already roused by a moment of her company. He had no idea if she was still upset by the kiss or because he'd concealed his profession, and he really had no time for complications of the fiery, blue-eyed variety. Except, the part of him that was just a man demanded that, for this particular woman, he *make* time.

'I know I should have mentioned that I'm a doctor last night,' he said as the lift arrived and the doors opened. 'I've just started a locum geriatrician position here.'

'Yes, you should.' She stepped inside. 'But, now that you've explained, I'll wish you a good day, doctor.'

Ducking inside the lift before the doors closed, Andreas continued, 'Listen, Clara, now that we're alone, I want to apologise again for last night.'

'Oh?' Completely unfazed, she glanced down her pert little nose at him, impressive given their height difference. It made him think of the Swedish term of endearment *sötnos*, the literal translation of which was 'sweet nose'.

'Don't worry.' She huffed, stabbing once more at the second-floor button as if her impatience alone could make the lift ascend faster. '*I* regret it too.'

She was so desperate to get away from him now.

Andreas inched closer and rested his gaze on that kissable mouth, now pinched with irritation. 'Oh, I don't regret the kissing for one second, *sötnos*.'

Alone with her in this confined space, there was no avoiding her bewitching scent or the erotic memories blasting him from all angles.

'I'm not your sweetie,' she snapped, flinging the endearment back in his face as if it were poison.

But her pupils dilated, her pulse flickered in her neck and her eyes dipped to his mouth every few seconds as if she too could remember every steamy detail of the night before.

'You might regret it now,' he taunted, 'But last night you enjoyed kissing me. I was there. I felt your body against mine, your fingers tugging at my hair…heard your sexy little whimpers.'

They had unfinished business.

'Maybe I did,' she admitted, planting her hands on her hips and leaning closer. 'But so did *you*.'

Andreas held up his hands in surrender. 'You'll get no argument from me. I wanted to kiss you the minute you laughed at me for hurling my leg.'

She huffed again, frustrated. 'But I didn't enjoy it enough to lose my job over or do it again.'

She was breathless now, her eyes ablaze with challenge and something else—something wild, reckless and needy that helped him to see the last lie for what it was.

But enough games; she might want nothing more to do with him when he told her his other secret.

Being a public figure came with complications that some people couldn't tolerate.

'And *that's* why I'm apologising,' he said, turning serious as guilt at his abuse of power sent chills down his spine. 'That you felt your job was at risk is unforgivable. I would never allow you to face repercussions when the kiss was fully my responsibility.'

Now he had her attention. She blinked, as if she was momentarily confused, then her stare hardened.

'Well, I hope you don't expect me to be grateful.' Her lip curled in distaste. 'Just because I've seen the goods...' her stare dipped to his groin '...doesn't mean I'm interested in making a purchase.'

When their eyes met again, he unleashed a victorious grin. If only she'd resisted checking him out last night when his towel had slipped, he might believe her now.

'I'd rather be homeless,' she continued, her colour high, her voice breathy. 'So, if you think I somehow owe you for your discretion, you can think again.'

Adrenaline rushed his system, urgent and fiery, compelling him to act. 'Exactly what kind of man do you think I am?' he asked, his voice deceptively calm despite the accusations she was hurling his way.

She obviously didn't trust him, but did she truly think him capable of blackmailing her into sex?

'I don't know you.' She raised her chin in defiance. 'So far, you've proved yourself utterly untrustworthy. You had a perfect opportunity to tell me you were a doctor last night, but you didn't. Even now when you've *come to explain*—' she made finger quotes '—you're being vague. Maybe you enjoyed misleading me. Maybe you're used to getting your own way and manipulating people. Maybe you expected a whole lot more than a kiss.'

At her goading, all his good intentions to make amends and come clean evaporated. If only she knew what he'd wanted in the moment when their tongues had been duelling, her luscious body restless against his, craving more. And, for all her denial, their undeniable magnetism was generating enough sparks to set the lift alight.

But maybe he'd been wrong about her; maybe he couldn't be the real Andreas with her after all.

'You're right—you *don't* know me,' he said, catching the sound of her sharply inhaled breath as his stare raked her features, from the icy chips in her irises to the plump fullness of those lovely lips. 'So let me enlighten you. I don't need to bribe or manipulate women into my bed. They come eagerly and leave satisfied.'

His heartbeat raced, thick arousal boiling in his belly.

'Oh, I bet they do.' She snorted in disgust. 'Well, *I* have no intention of being one of those women.'

But she was panting hard and had stepped up close, raising her face to his so one mutual move would send them back into each other's arms.

'Are you sure about that, *sötnos*?' he asked lazily. 'Because you're looking at me like I'm the last cookie in the jar again.'

But he needed to master their chemistry, and fast. With her two jobs, she'd be everywhere he looked. Just as she knew nothing about him, he knew little about her beyond her education and employment history. Nothing about the things that counted: her integrity, her moral compass, her loyalty.

His public position necessitated discretion in the people he invited into his life, even casually. And, while it was perfectly acceptable for hospital staff to fraternise, he still hadn't explained the small detail of his royal life. Would she treat him differently when she knew that he was Varborg's heir that should never have been?

Just then, while they faced each other, eyes locked in challenge, the lift arrived on the staff-only floor.

The doors slid open, breaking the sexually charged impasse.

Andreas stepped back, breathing through the wild thudding of his heart. How had the conversation veered in a completely tangential direction from the one he'd planned? What was it about this woman that left him struggling to walk away? And what had caused her distrust and general cynicism towards men, when it was obvious to anyone with eyes how hot they were for each other?

Waiting outside the lift slightly out of breath, as if he'd taken the stairs at full pelt, was Andreas's bodyguard, Nils.

'Your Highness, there's been a security breach

in the emergency department.' Nils flicked a brief look at Clara who, as a staff member both at Nordic Care and at the palace, would be well known to the security team that monitored Andreas's every move. 'You need to come with me now, sir.'

Defeat rumbled in Andreas's chest. He winced as he took in Clara's stunned confusion.

'Who's this?' she asked, her jaw dropping. 'And what did he just call you?'

She'd made it perfectly clear today that she had little trust for him, and now he'd missed the opportunity to have her hear the news from him direct.

'Give me a moment,' Andreas instructed Nils, who dutifully stepped aside out of earshot.

Andreas turned to Clara, his control of the situation now tugged like a rug from under his feet. If she'd wanted nothing more to do with him when she'd thought he was just a man who'd failed to declare his profession, his royal baggage, the ultimate complication, would likely be the final straw. It shouldn't matter. He'd come back to Varborg for family reasons, not for fun. Except that addictive lure of being just himself with this woman was hard to fight.

Taking Clara's elbow, he led her into an alcove beside the lifts. 'This is why I wanted to speak with you. I intended to explain my...heritage, my role at the palace...but then we got side-tracked again.'

He dropped his hand, instantly missing the feel of her silky skin beneath his fingertips, more off-kilter than ever with her this close physically, while emotionally he could literally see her slipping further away.

As if she'd finally pieced the jigsaw together, her hand covered her mouth, horrified. 'This isn't a joke. You're really a prince…?'

'I'm afraid so.'

What he wouldn't give to be just a doctor in that moment, to have her look at him the way she had last night, right before that kiss. He could escape for ever in eyes like hers. But escape wasn't an option.

'I thought you were familiar… But you're a doctor,' she said, clearly trying to make sense of the scattered pieces of information, the panicked tone of her voice telling him all he needed to know about her current regrets. 'You were staying in the guest wing.'

Andreas sighed, resigned. 'I refused to occupy the suite prepared for me in the family wing.' He swallowed, forcing himself to continue. 'It once belonged to my brother.'

Andreas had a hard enough time with his grief, and unfavourably comparing himself to Oscar, without occupying his rooms.

'And I've grown used to sparse but comfortable doctor's digs at hospitals,' he finished, braced for her transformation as reality sunk in.

Last night, when she'd blasted into his predictable, privileged life like a tornado—and again this morning, while they'd worked together to treat their patient—he'd foolishly clung to the hope of something real and unguarded with this exceptional woman he couldn't seem to forget.

But, now that she knew the truth, he would no longer be just Andreas the man and doctor, in her eyes. He would be something else—something two-dimensional, a caricature.

'You let me believe you were a nobody...' She scowled and shook her head, as if dazed. 'I kissed a prince...?'

She might as well have said she'd kissed a frog for all the contempt with which she spoke his title.

'Oh, don't worry.' Desire heated his blood as he stepped closer and watched her eyes widen, her breath catch and arousal flush her skin. 'Prince or not, I remember every second of our kiss and, what's more, so do you.'

'I do...' She blinked up at him, clearly stunned into an honest admission. 'But I'm sorry—it won't happen again.'

Hot, sharp jealousy sliced through him. 'So you were willing to flirt with me and kiss me when you assumed me to be a guest of the royal family but, now you know I'm Prince Henrik's son, you want nothing more to do with me—is that it?'

Futility stiffened his muscles. Part of him, the same part that refused to give up his career until he had no choice, refused to accept that the fantasy of this woman was over. He wanted to remind her of the inferno they'd generated when they'd been in each other's arms, him naked and her wild for him.

'I…' Her mortified stare darted to Nils. 'Can't we just forget it happened?' she snapped.

Andreas raised his brows dubiously. 'We could try and forget, if that's what you want.'

Ever since Oscar's death, what Andreas wanted, be it his medical career or the woman who now seemed horrified by his true identity, hadn't been his choice to make. And, when it came to this woman and the kind of chemistry they shared, forgetting the way she'd looked at him with heat and desire would be an uphill challenge.

But he would have to find a way to work alongside her until it was time for him to hang up his stethoscope for good.

Sensing Nils' urgency, he tilted his head with regret, his duty to his family tugging him away.

'Either way, we'll need to talk about the kissing some other time,' he said. 'I must go.'

Taking one last look at her, he took out his frustration on the stairs as he headed for the armoured vehicle awaiting him outside.

CHAPTER FIVE

TWO DAYS LATER, Clara returned to the palace for her next night shift, her stomach twisted into knots of dread and humiliation. Half of her was desperate to avoid seeing Andreas again—*Prince* Andreas—the other half had no idea what she wanted, beyond wishing she could turn back time and never have met him in the first place. How dared he flirt with her twice, but keep such an important identity a secret?

Following the footman to Prince Henrik's private rooms, her face heated with the memory of how she'd snogged, ogled and then insulted the heir to the throne. She stifled a snort of disbelief. Her actions had been bad enough when she'd assumed Andreas was a hunky diplomat and then a doctor.

Now, she was so confused, because Andreas was right—she *did* recall every thrilling second of that kiss and she had no hope of forgetting. She might not trust him, but her body didn't seem to care that, for a woman like Clara, an ordinary nobody with financial woes and a notorious convicted conman for a father, he was the most ridiculously out-of-reach man in the universe.

She had such little experience with relationships, thanks to Lars and those lost teenage years and thanks to the guy who'd taken her virginity and then acted as if they were strangers. Her attraction to Andreas of all men was...laughable.

The only sensible course of action was to keep her distance. No more lusting after him, no more bickering and no more reliving his look of defeat when he'd accused her of wanting nothing more to do with him.

Resolved, Clara waited while the footman tapped quietly on the door. She dragged in a shaky breath, preparing herself to finally meet her patient, Andreas's father. After signing her confidentiality agreement on the first night, she'd been given the prince's medical records.

The prognosis wasn't good. After a short battle with prostate cancer, Prince Henrik had recently been diagnosed with stage four disease and was currently undergoing a course of radiotherapy for painful bone metastases.

Clara's heart ached for the older man, and for Andreas. Having nursed her mother through breast cancer treatment a few years ago, she knew exactly what the family was going through—although Andreas had shown no obvious signs that he was even aware that his father's disease was terminal, beyond stating that he was both a doctor and a diplomat *for the time being*.

Had that cryptic reference been because he knew he would soon need to forgo his medical career and succeed his father? Compassion clenched her heart. She understood how it felt to be tugged in all directions. She'd just started her nursing degree when Alma Lund had been diagnosed. Clara had considered dropping out to care for her mother full time, but fortunately her mother wouldn't hear of it. At least Clara had been able to continue with her career, her independence invaluable, whereas Andreas would likely have no choice but to give up medicine. He couldn't rule Varborg *and* work at the hospital.

The door opened. Prince Henrik's private butler appeared and quietly ushered Clara inside.

'His majesty is uncomfortable tonight and cannot sleep,' the man she'd been informed was named Møller said, his face etched in concern. 'I believe his pain management requires addressing.'

Clara nodded, trying to shove her patient's son from her mind. But she couldn't seem to block out the vulnerability she'd seen in his eyes when he'd accused her of treating him differently because he'd grown up here, surrounded by wealth and privilege.

Why had that look of defeat in Andreas's eyes called to her on such a profound level? Was it just that, for all their differences, she could empathise with him both about his father's illness and the loss of his career? Or was the idea he might be torn between his two roles deeply unsettling? She shook her head, disgusted with herself. How did all roads lead back to Andreas?

She followed Møller's stiff gait through a series of ante rooms, her nerves growing with every step. But the prince was a patient like any other; all Clara needed to do was her job.

They arrived outside another door and the butler knocked, waiting to be admitted into what Clara soon saw was the prince's private sitting room.

The man sat in an arm chair before a sleek contemporary fireplace built into a marble surround. Clara approached and curtseyed, as she'd been taught, waiting for Prince Henrik to address her first.

'Your name is Clara?' he asked, his face pale, his eyes red with fatigue.

'Yes, Your Highness.'

She'd seen him a handful of times in the media. His head was on Varborg's stamps and coins. But in person it was the likeness to his virile, handsome son that made Clara's heart gallop with longing to see Andreas again.

Huh! Her resolve clearly meant nothing...

But how could she ignore the prince she'd kissed—the man to whom, for all her denials, she was obviously still drawn—when his life was about to change irrevocably because his father was terminally ill?

'Can I help you, sir?' Clara stepped closer, urged by the butler, who then discreetly left the room.

'I'm in pain,' the prince said. 'My bones ache and this blasted thing isn't working.'

He indicated the syringe driver strapped to his arm, which had been prescribed to administer analgesia while he was undergoing treatment.

'Can I examine your arm, sir?' Empathy for the

older man, a man from whom Andreas had inherited his grey-blue eyes, tugged at her heartstrings.

Varborg's ruler was beloved by the nation. For fifty years he'd ruled with diligence and dignity, despite his share of adversity—losing his wife when his sons had been teenagers and, more recently, his oldest son, Oscar. If only she'd done her homework on her patient's past sooner, she might have recognised Andreas.

Prince Henrik nodded and slipped his arm free of his blue velvet dressing gown. Focussed on her work, and not the tragic losses of Varborg's royal family, Clara peeled away the dressing from the needle site, finding an angry red patch of skin where the cannula had extravasated.

'I'm afraid it's slipped out.' She disposed of the cannula in the nearby sharps bin. 'I'll need to re-site the needle, if that's okay.'

'Of course, dear. I'm pretty much a pin cushion at this stage,' he said with a sad smile that gave his stare the same aching vulnerability she'd witnessed in Andreas. Did these two proud men know how similar they were?

Trying not to think about his deceptive son, Clara pulled on gloves and grabbed a fresh subcutaneous cannula, some antiseptic wipes and a new adhesive dressing.

'I hear you've met my son,' the prince said, watching her with shrewd eyes that spoke of sharp intelligence and an ability to read people easily.

'I have. We work together at Nordic Care.' Clara willed herself not to blush.

While she held this prestigious position she couldn't expect to have any secrets. She only hoped that the prince was unaware of her late-night antics with his naked son.

In the days since she'd discovered Andreas's true identity, she'd scoured the Internet for any information she could find on Europe's most eligible and unusual prince. There'd been tales of his military career, his work as a doctor and photographs of his playboy antics—an immaculately dressed Andreas attending various glitzy functions accompanied by a string of beautiful society women. The latter had caused such searing jealousy, she'd had to slam closed her laptop in disgust.

'Ah, yes, the day job…' Prince Henrik sighed and closed his eyes as Clara cleaned a patch of skin on his arm with the antiseptic wipes. 'Tell me, is he a good doctor?'

'Yes,' she said simply, recalling the way they'd worked together to revive Mr Engman. 'He's very well respected. A favourite with the patients, I'm told.' Many of whom had volunteered to Clara what a compassionate and caring man they found the heir to the throne; how natural and grounded he appeared to his patients, treating them with empathy and respect.

But why was the prince asking *her*, the palace's newest member of staff? Surely he and Andreas spoke about his work?

'Just a small scratch now, sir,' she said, burning up with questions about their relationship she would never dare to ask. At Prince Henrik's silent nod, Clara inserted the subcutaneous needle just beneath the skin, securing it with the dressing. Then she reattached the syringe driver and adjusted the dose of pain killers.

She shouldn't care what kind of relationship Andreas had with his dying father *or* whom he dated. He was handsome, intelligent and a *prince*: of course he was a catch for any woman willing to forgo her independence and put *his* life first.

Intense chemistry or not, that woman wasn't Clara.

For all her father's faults, Alma had loved Lars Lund. Young Clara had loved him too, craving his attention. But, where her mother had forgiven him countless times for his erratic employment history and excused his unreliability, teenaged Clara had grown more and more wary with each disappointment. She'd seen the fallout and had witnessed Alma struggling to put on a brave face when Lars had lost yet another job, or pretend all was well when the electricity had been cut off. Clara had been the one taking care of Freja after school while Alma had worked longer hours. She'd understood that her parents' marriage was unequal; that loving the wrong man, having his children, had left Alma vulnerable.

Even after her father had left for good to pursue his dubious, get-rich-quick schemes, the final one sending him to prison, he'd burdened the family with deeper debt. It wasn't until after his death that Clara's mother had discovered he'd re-mortgaged the house.

'We don't get on terribly well, my son and I,' Prince Henrik said, taking her by surprise.

He opened his shrewd eyes and Clara froze, uncertain how to reply. But her curiosity for Andreas went wild. The more she learned about the man behind the headlines, the harder it was to ignore him the way she wanted to.

'He resents me, you see,' the older man said, as if to himself, his stare far away. 'I've reminded him of his birth right and his responsibilities to the crown.'

Without comment, Clara silently disposed of her gloves.

She had no idea how Andreas felt about anything, his relationship with his father and his crown prince duties included. They were virtual strangers.

She understood complex relationships, having experienced years of rejection and disappointment with her own untrustworthy father. But, whereas Lars had passed away while serving his sentence for fraud before Clara had had a chance to face him with some home truths, at least *this* father and son still had time to air their grievances and reconcile their differences.

But not much time.

'Are you feeling more comfortable now, sir?' Clara stooped at the prince's side, adjusting the blanket across his knees. His eyes had fallen closed once more, the tension around his mouth easing as the pain medication began to work.

'I gave him too much freedom when he was younger, you see...' he continued. 'I allowed the boy to choose a career for himself, when perhaps I should have had greater expectations of him as a prince.'

Clara's skin prickled with discomfort, as if she were eavesdropping. Patients voiced all sorts of things in their most vulnerable moments. Part of her wanted to leave the prince to his privacy but, if he wanted to talk as her patient, she would listen.

'I promised his mother before she died that I would allow the boys to have as normal a life as possible...' He was slurring now, obviously on the cusp of sleep. 'It wasn't always possible for Oscar, but with Andreas... I tried my best, but I missed their mother, so very much...'

Compassion squeezed Clara's heart. She blinked away the sting in her eyes, recalling the stark terror she'd experienced on more than one occasion when she imagined losing her mother. Prince Henrik was a man like any other. He was still grieving for his wife and wondering if he'd been a good enough father to his sons. Like many families, Varborg's first family had their issues, for all their power and privilege.

In desperation, Clara cast around for sight of the butler lurking in a doorway. Perhaps together they could encourage the prince back to bed. Spying a call button next to the prince's arm chair, Clara gave it the briefest of pushes, hoping it wouldn't sound in the room and wake the dozing man.

Within seconds, the butler appeared. Clara explained the issue with the syringe driver, keeping the man's privileged confessions to herself. But, as she made her way back to the staff sitting-room, her feet dragged, her heart heavy.

The more she learned about Andreas, the murkier the picture that emerged. Did he resent his father for calling him back to Varborg? Did he know the prince was terminally ill? That would surely devastate him; and how would he feel, having to give up his career as a doctor?

But the hardest question of all to answer was why she cared so much when she'd vowed to keep him at arm's length.

CHAPTER SIX

THE EMBOSSED AND gilded envelope had arrived the following day—an invitation to Prince Henrik's private Jubilee Banquet, an intimate celebration of his fifty years on the throne.

When the gown box had been delivered shortly afterwards, she'd assumed that the formal wear was part of the clothing allowance that came with her salary. She hadn't been able to resist peeling back the layers of gossamer tissue paper and trying on the most extravagant garment she'd ever handled... just once.

And now, three days later, she was wearing the gown for real—a black, lace beaded sheath that clung to her body and flared at her feet, her heart beating into her throat with awe as she was ushered inside an opulent banquet hall in the formal and ceremonial wing of the palace.

Clara swallowed, any ridiculous fantasy that she and Andreas might have anything in common, or that he needed *her* concern, crushed into the plush carpet so thick she could have been walking on a cloud.

This part of the winter residence was often open to the public, but tonight it glittered in celebration. The cold marble of the columns and ornate cornices was warmed by the six enormous chandeliers that hung from the ceiling, as well as a million twinkling lights strung like a net of stars across the night sky. To one side, row after row of banquet tables were precisely laid with glittering crystal glassware, ornate gilded centrepieces and cascading fresh flower arrangements. A chamber orchestra occupied a raised dais, where guests danced to ballroom versions of popular Scandinavian folk songs.

Utterly overwhelmed, Clara slipped discreetly around the edge of the room, hoping to blend into the gold-edged midnight-blue drapes that lined the walls, stretching from the floor to the vaulted ceiling.

She scanned the room, casually searching out her nursing colleagues among the Varborg elite. Her pulse fluttered frantically, her body hopeful, her mind full of dread.

Was *he* there—Prince Andreas?

She hadn't seen him since the day she'd discovered his identity. That had left plenty of time to promise that, next time they met, she would keep things strictly professional and properly deferential.

She'd just spied her nursing colleagues on the other side of the dance floor when her stare landed on the hottest man in any room.

Andreas.

She froze. Her mouth dried. She couldn't look away as euphoria spiked her blood. How had she ever once mistaken him for an ordinary man? He'd been utterly spectacular naked, seriously sexy in his hospital scrubs but, dressed in his formal attire, he looked every inch an untouchable heartthrob prince.

Desire, thick, hot and confusing, pounded through her veins.

An impressive row of medals adorned the lapel of his dark tailcoat, the breast pocket bearing the Cronstedt royal coat of arms. His crisp white dress-shirt and waistcoat contrasted with the midnight-blue sash worn across his broad chest, the colour complementing his mesmerising eyes. Nearly every other man there was clean-shaven but, unlike them, he wore his beard, neatly trimmed short, and his golden hair swept back from his aristocratic face, just an inch too long so the ends curled above his collar.

A true, unapologetic Viking.

Horribly turned on, Clara sank deeper into the shadows. Why did her treacherous body hate her so much, when her head had already made all the decisions? She gripped the folds of velvet, wishing she could disappear into the curtains so she wouldn't have to witness him sharing that dazzling smile of his with the stunning and elegant society women who, unlike Clara, were a part of his world.

Moving on from one conversation, Andreas addressed the mountain of a man at his side—Nils, the bodyguard from the hospital—before conversing with a regal blonde wearing a tiara made of diamonds that Clara would bet a year's salary were real.

Clara's skin prickled with humiliation. Here, in

Andreas's world, she was so utterly and obviously out of her depth, an imposter in a hired gown.

Nils spoke into a discreet microphone attached to the earpiece he was wearing, his stare landing on Clara across the vast room, as if he'd just been informed of her precise location.

Clara froze. Would she be told to leave in front of all these important people? In front of *him*? Perhaps it wasn't too late to duck out before Andreas saw her. She should never have come. She couldn't face him. He would surely see through her disguise to the scared little girl inside who'd been abandoned by one parent and forced to grow up fast to help care for the other. What would Crown Prince Andreas Cronstedt need with a woman like that when he could kiss any woman he chose?

The bodyguard whispered to Andreas. With a charming smile, Andreas concluded his conversation with a portly man in his sixties, turned and stared straight at Clara.

A soft gasp left her dry throat.

He'd asked Nils about *her*; the room was obviously awash with his spies.

From so far away, she couldn't read his expression. Was he annoyed to see her there after their childish squabble in the lift? What on earth did it matter who regretted the kiss, who'd enjoyed it, who recalled every detail when it was unlikely ever to happen again?

Desperately clinging to the indifference she'd spent days perfecting, Clara raised her chin and gripped her clutch, which contained her embossed invitation, like a shield.

Without taking his eyes off hers for one second, Andreas marched her way.

Her palms began to sweat.

His long strides sliced through the parting crowd.

Her ears buzzed with tinnitus.

Still he descended, full of purpose and so achingly beautiful, looking at him stung Clara's eyes.

People had started to notice his determined trajectory. Clara grew hot under their curious stares. Whispers began to spread from person to person like a highly contagious virus. Clara's pulse throbbed frantically in her fingertips and toes. Her head grew light from lack of oxygen. She gulped down a few breaths, trying to look away from his intense eye contact, but she couldn't make her body obey her commands. Was this what a stroke felt like? She could only stand and wait for him to arrive, her only armour her determination to stay immune to his overwhelming magnetism.

'You made it,' he said with a small, restrained smile.

He seemed taller and broader in his exquisitely tailored attire, every inch the regal, self-assured leader he was born to be.

Ignoring his devastating hotness, Clara lowered her gaze. 'Your Royal Highness.'

Her voice croaked as she bent her knees in the deep curtsey she'd been practising in her heels and gown all afternoon.

All around them, people were staring, likely thinking who exactly could have inspired Prince Andreas's inexhaustible pursuit across a room full of important people who, like him, belonged there.

When she looked up, Andreas's mouth wore a tight smile and his eyes were grey and stormy with what looked like fury.

'Please *never* do that again,' he said, his voice low for her ears only.

Clara blinked up at him, a barrage of questions and comments dying on her tongue. How did he expect her to act? She hadn't been trained on the proper etiquette for addressing a prince you'd kissed, seen naked and then tried to ignore. But there was no time to wonder what social *faux pas* she'd made.

He held out his hand. 'Ms Lund, would you do me the honour of a dance?'

Clara quailed inside, dread freezing her diamanté-clad feet to the lush carpet. She had no idea how to dance to this kind of music. She'd make a fool of herself and, worse, a fool of him in a room full of his snobby, aristocratic peers.

She opened her mouth, praying that it wouldn't be considered an act of high treason to politely refuse a crown prince a dance, when Andreas spoke again.

'Before you decline…' he angled his head closer '…shall I remind you that we agreed to talk about a certain, very pressing matter?'

He was so calm, so composed, they might have been discussing the weather. But surely they couldn't settle their unfinished business, *the kissing*, in front of all these people?

Clara's entire body burned hot, her skin hyper-sensitised under his observation. She could barely stand upright just thinking about the heat, fizz and excitement of that kiss. Just looking at him all dressed up made that reckless, carefree part of her that felt alive every time she talked to him ache to do it again.

'Your Royal Highness,' she said, placing her hand in his, 'I merely hoped to spare you the public spectacle of me treading on your toes. I have no idea how to dance like this.'

'I'll lead you,' he said, self-assured, smiling at several of the gawking crowd. 'Just keep your eyes on mine.'

The onlookers parted for them as, unconcerned, Andreas led her to the dance floor. He executed a short bow, gripped her hand and placed his other hand between her shoulder blades. 'Allow me to worry what your feet are doing.'

'That's easy for you to say,' Clara muttered, her body melting under his touch. 'But I much prefer to rely on my own two feet.'

Before she could make further complaints, he swept her along into the dancing crowd. Clara gasped, the thrill of once more being this close to him rendering her speechless. The warmth of his body seeped into her palm where it rested on his shoulder. The spicy scent of his cologne, delicious notes of pine forest and wood smoke, sent her head swimming back to fantasy land. The all-consuming focus of his eye contact made her forget that she was being watched by hundreds of onlookers as he effortlessly spun her in time to the music, his strong arms and skilled dance moves preventing her from taking a wrong step.

She laughed, the thrilling abandon of dancing with so expert a partner suppressing her reservations and insecurities. She might as well have been flying. Andreas grinned at her delight, spinning her a little faster so the hem of her dress fanned out, holding her a little closer so she was forced to surrender her body and dignity to him entirely, the way she'd surrendered to that kiss.

Alive once more, all she could do was smile. But this wasn't reality. Reality was her bank balance; the shameful online headlines bearing her family name; the sting of humiliation she'd experienced outside the hospital lift, when she'd realised with a sinking stomach that, no matter what her body craved, him and her could never be.

As the tempo of the music slowed, she felt Andreas's body stiffen a little, as if he was aware of the change in her mood.

'I want to apologise for rushing off that day at the hospital. I'm afraid that, no matter how much I value my work, I must put my family first.'

Clara gave a small sharp shake of her head, stunned by the regret in his voice, the implication that Prince Henrik was right—their relationship was strained. 'There's no need to apologise, Your Royal

Highness. I'm embarrassed that I didn't know you straight away when you're so...famous.'

His fingers flexed against her bare back, or she might have imagined it, because he looked perfectly polite, no hint of the heat from that first night.

But what did she expect—that she, ordinary Clara Lund, was special? Maybe he wanted to explain that, given his wild and notorious past, he kissed everyone he met that way...

'You accused me of manipulation.' His jaw clenched. 'But the truth is, when you didn't recognise me, I found the anonymity liberating. You fascinated me, with your hair primly pinned back but with your bold and spunky attitude on display.'

Clara exhaled a sound of disbelief as shameful prickles of heat danced over her skin. 'I'm outspoken. The way I spoke to you must be an act of treason. Not to mention the...kissing.' She hissed the last word. 'Two hundred years ago I'd have probably been imprisoned or sent to the guillotine.'

He smiled, a glimmer of playfulness in his eyes that unfurled something deep inside her—that longing to be the young woman she was in years. Clara wished they were at work, where at least she could pretend they were equals, but here, among the glitz and glamour, the titles and ceremony, it was obvious that they had nothing in common.

'You weren't outspoken, you were honest. That hardly ever happens to me. I've never met a woman like you.' He sobered. 'In truth, I was struggling to be back here that night. Just for a few moments, I wanted to just be myself with you. Selfish, I know.'

Why was he struggling to be home? Was it the prince's diagnosis and his regrets over his career? And couldn't he be himself with everyone? Hadn't she felt the same? For a few moments in his company, she'd felt more vibrantly alive than she'd ever felt before.

'And I guarantee that, these days...' his lips twitched with amusement '...kissing a prince carries no such penalty.'

In spite of the confusing mix of desire and unease swirling inside her, Clara laughed. If only they were alone, they could have a candid conversation and get to know each other better. Discover if they had other things in common.

Ridiculous! He was a prince. They weren't on a date. He probably had official duties tonight, given that Prince Henrik was, as yet, nowhere to be seen. And she was out of her depth. Feeling foolish at how easily she'd been seduced to feel emotionally close to a man who was from another world, Clara changed the subject.

'You look very...regal. Did you earn all those medals?'

'Yes,' he stated simply, obviously reluctant to talk about his military service. 'You look beautiful in that dress,' he said instead. 'I knew it would suit you.'

Clara stiffened, her confusion growing. '*You* picked out this dress?'

He gave a half-shrug, as if the gesture was no big deal.

'Why?' Something spiky and hard settled in her stomach. She was so naïve.

'I thought you'd like it.' A frown tugged down his beautiful mouth. 'Consider it a gift—an apology for making you feel that your job here was compromised by my actions.'

Clara's throat burned with humiliation. Of course he wouldn't understand the symbolism of what for him was a seemingly innocent gesture.

Seeing red, Clara hardened her stare. 'Well, then, I insist on paying you back.'

As if the dress was tainted, her skin began to chafe and itch underneath.

He maintained his bland smile but a muscle ticked in his jaw. 'That's not necessary.'

'It's necessary to *me*.' A flush crept up her neck. 'I don't like to be beholden to anyone. I pay my own way in the world.'

Chills rattled her bones. She shouldn't have come tonight. She didn't belong here, not like this: pretending to fit in, wearing a borrowed dress, playing Cinderella in his arms when any second now the clock would strike midnight and he'd see how implausible their flirtation was.

'Why so independent, *sötnos*?' He gripped her waist a little tighter, as if he could literally repair the damage he would never understand by holding onto her. 'I simply assumed you might find the gift welcome. After all, you work so hard.'

Shaking her head with disbelief, Clara forced her feet to remember that they were under her own control, not his. 'That's an easy thing for you to ask when you grew up here. But seeing as you appreciate my candour, Your Royal Highness, know this: I've been contributing to my family's income since I was sixteen and my father upped and left us with nothing but his debts, never to return.'

Stricken, Andreas appeared instantly contrite, but it was little comfort.

'I'm sorry,' he said, a flicker of panic in his stare. 'Please accept my apologies for the dress. It won't happen again.'

Appalled by the burn of irrational tears behind her eyes, Clara tried to remove her hand from his.

She *never* cried.

'I should have known,' she said, shaking her head when he refused to relinquish his grip, the panic in his eyes now full-blown.

She wouldn't make a scene, but nor would she play his puppet, regardless of their audience.

'For a minute there,' she continued, 'I'd almost convinced myself that we were, in some ways, equals. That we had something important in common. But the cold hard reality is that I was fooling myself.'

His stare turned steely, the muscles of his clenched jaw standing out beneath his facial hair. 'We *are* equals. Two human beings drawn to each other.'

Clara scoffed at his naïvety.

'Are we?' She fought to keep her voice as calm and quiet as she could, given the humiliation pounding in her head. 'In that case, what's it to be? Repayment for the dress? Or do you prefer I return the garment? I can take it off right now, in fact.'

Indignant, she skidded her feet to a halt and reached for the side zip under her arm.

Andreas's eyes blazed with an inferno of heat.

'Don't you dare,' he growled, taking her arm.

With a benign smile on his face, he guided her from the dance floor and through an inconspicuous door tucked into the corner, manned by two liveried footmen.

Awash with shame for her outburst—and spitting mad that, for all her independence and distrust, she'd been naïve enough to fall under his spell out there on the dance floor—Clara accepted her fate. She'd done it now; he would kick her out and wash his hands of her.

And it would be for the best. She was so laughably out of her depth in his world. Their stark differences had only been highlighted by the extravagance of the stupidly beautiful dress that now felt like a prison straitjacket.

But, for one heady moment out there in his arms, as he'd twirled her round and round, nothing else had seemed to matter—not his title, or her family debts, or even the misguided attraction she just couldn't seem to fight. He'd been just a man, and she a woman.

Except when the dancing had stopped, and her

feet were firmly back on the ground, reality had struck. They came from impossibly different worlds: his full of glitter and magic, and hers the real world.

CHAPTER SEVEN

LENGTHENING HIS STRIDE, Andreas ducked into the nearby Blue Room, his blood on fire. From the minute he'd spied Clara from across the ballroom, the sophisticated black lace gown he'd chosen hugging the curves of her sensational body like a glove, he'd been deafened by a roar of desire. As he'd crossed the endless-seeming distance between them, urgency had pounded through his head. He'd wanted to blindfold every other man present. Better still, he should have called off the banquet, sent everyone home and selfishly had her to himself.

Except she didn't want him…

The door closed behind them—no doubt Nils's doing, so he could stand sentry.

Clara tugged her hand from his. Reeling from the loss of her touch and the tightness gripping his insides like a fist, he scrubbed a hand through his hair.

'What are you trying to do to me?' His breathing turned harsh as he fought for the control that had seemed second nature to him until he'd met this woman. 'Threatening to take off that dress?'

As if of its own accord, his frantic stare traced her lush curves, the cascading lace no barrier to his vivid and debauched imagination about what delights lay underneath.

'You should have asked someone else to dance,' she snapped, ignoring the reference to their chemistry. 'I told you I couldn't do it.'

'You did it just fine, until you stopped trusting me. And I wanted to dance with you, *sötnos*.'

He paced closer, catching the sparks of hurt in her eyes. 'This isn't about dancing or dresses,' he said, shame thickening his voice. 'I hurt you.'

She pressed her lovely lips together and hid her eyes from him by looking down.

'I'm sorry,' he said. 'I hate that I let you down over something that looks so beautiful. If I'd known how...insulting you would find the gesture, I never would have done it.'

Guilt punched him in the gut, its force no match for the arousal coiled in his belly because she was close, so close, her scent bewitching.

'All I seem to do is apologise.' He scrubbed a hand down his face. He'd crossed the line and been selfish and entitled. He should never have asked her to dance, because the minute he'd taken her in his arms he'd no longer been able to pretend that he had their chemistry under control. When she'd talked about removing the dress, vulnerable but defiant before him, he'd almost fallen to his knees.

But he needed to grapple back control. He didn't want to hurt her more than he had already. He didn't want to let her down the way she'd obviously been let down before by her father.

'It doesn't matter.' She looked down and Andreas wanted to punch something—preferably himself.

'It matters to *me*.' He paced away in frustration, spinning to face her once more. 'I got carried away. I thought we made a connection. But then you seemed disgusted by my title. I told myself I would leave you alone, but then I learned you'd been invited tonight. I saw that dress and imagined you in it and then you came, wearing it, looking stunning, the only person in the room I genuinely wanted to see.'

She frowned, confused.

'Why me?' she asked, as fearless as ever. 'When you had that entire room to choose from, every other woman more on your level than I will ever be, no matter how fancy you dress me up?'

She was right: they were from different backgrounds. She had her own demons—financial strains and trust issues he knew nothing about. By asking her to dance, by dragging her into the goldfish bowl of his life, he'd surely exposed her to the rife speculation that would follow—the last thing she deserved. He'd have to spend the remainder of the evening running damage limitation—playing the playboy prince of old, dancing with every single woman in the room in order to head off the gossips and society bloodhounds who always seemed to bay for his blood. Andreas the stand-in—never more so than tonight, when his father, the man they'd all assembled to celebrate, was indisposed with a bad headache.

His first public appearance for his father and he'd messed up. But, as long as he lived, he would never regret it fully. For a brief time, when she'd trusted him on the dance floor, he'd felt invincible with her in his arms.

'Because I'm selfish, okay?' Andreas winced, hating that he'd made her feel so small. 'The fact that you're different, that you don't seem to care about all of this—' he waved his arm to encompass the ornate room in which they stood, the vast banquet hall beyond, the very palace itself '—is what I like about you. I wanted you, grounding me the way you did that first night when you reminded me that—away from perceptions and duty to my family, away from the shoes of my dead brother that I must one day fill—sometimes I can just be myself: the real Andreas.'

Clara hesitated, her stare softening. 'And who is the real Andreas? The compassionate doctor taking the frail hand of an elderly patient? Or is he the party prince in those pictures on the Internet, invited to all the best gatherings, usually with some glamorous woman on his arm?'

'I admit, I've been both in my time.' Fascinated by her thrilling jealousy, he stepped closer and watched her breathing speed up, caught the enticing waft of her perfume that almost made his eyes roll closed in ecstasy. 'Are you jealous, *sötnos*?'

His blood surged at her sense of possession. She might feel that they came from different worlds, but she couldn't conceal how she felt physically. She wanted him in return—man, doctor and prince.

'Not at all,' she bluffed, clearing her throat in a

nervous gesture. 'I'm just disorientated, wondering what I'm doing here, how I should address you—or if I should even acknowledge you at all, given that we're from such starkly different worlds and clearly have *nothing* in common.'

'You can call me Andreas,' he said, ignoring the parts of her argument he deemed irrelevant as he focussed on her parted lips, slicked by some berry-coloured gloss he wanted more than anything to taste.

Oh, how he wanted to hear his name on her lips—preferably cried out in passion. But, now that she knew his true identity, would she give him her honest desire, as she had that first night? Or would she demure like a timid mouse simply because he'd been born into an historic family, something over which he'd had no control?

Clara licked her lips, as if aware of his observation and the direction of his thoughts. 'That hardly seems reverential enough, given the circumstances.'

Stepping closer, he drew her stare back to his, finding it full of her signature defiance. Triumph electrified his nerve endings at the resolute tilt of her chin. Clara was no mouse.

'That is exactly why I insist on it. When I'm with you, I'm just me. *You* are the one person I can rely on to treat me with brutal honesty. Don't turn on me now, *sötnos*, when I need an ally within these walls more than ever.'

He caught her soft gasp of astonishment and

watched as her pupils dilated and compassion re-placed all that fire in her eyes.

'Why do you need an ally in your family home?' she asked in a confused whisper, voicing the one question designed to strip him bare of his layers of armour. '*You* belong here.'

Andreas swallowed and tugged at the hem of his waistcoat, a reminder that he at least looked the part he'd been born to play. Except he'd spent most of his adult life free to live another role, to forge his own path, to just be a man who belonged in Clara's world.

'I do,' he agreed, desperate to talk about anything other than his royal life with this woman he wanted so badly, he could taste it. 'But I wasn't born the heir, wasn't raised for the position. So you see there are many out there, perhaps my father included, who believe I'm not fit to follow him to the throne. That it should have been my elder brother Oscar standing here today, charming the crowds and dancing with the most beautiful woman in the room.'

As the ugly truth spilled free, he glanced away from her frowning face, jealousy a hot slash through his chest at the idea of Clara dancing with the brother he'd loved. Should he also spill at her feet his guilt and regrets over Oscar's death? His secret fear that those with no confidence in him were right because, as a doctor and brother, he'd failed Oscar so completely?

No; he wanted her too much to risk it.

'That's not true,' she whispered, horrified.

'Isn't it?' he asked. 'I'm the spare, don't forget. My father certainly made that clear while I was growing up.'

'Is that why you refused your brother's rooms—why you're still in the guest wing? Perhaps you should talk to your father about this. Perhaps you're wrong about his reasons and how he feels.'

She reached for his arm, bringing him back from a dark place with her touch. But it was too much; it caught him off-guard, the desire that was never far away since that first night a roar in his head.

'While I appreciate your directness, *sötnos*, and your suggestions, do we know each other well enough for such advice? Because I might be prompted to ask why you work two jobs when one is all anyone could expect, or why you insist on paying your father's debts.'

She flushed but held her ground. 'Helping out my family financially is *my* choice.'

'As is choosing to forge my own path rather than stepping into my dead brother's shoes. But we don't always get what we want, do we? Sometimes, we must be something others need us to be.'

Clara's eyes widened, as if his words resonated deeply.

'Still think we have little in common?' he asked while they faced each other at an impasse, equals with, he suspected, more similarities than they had differences. Except, unlike him, she was free to choose how to live her life. He'd long ago come to terms with his...mostly.

Sighing with defeat, Andreas again rubbed a hand down his face.

'I asked you to dance so I could clear the air,' he said, his hands itching to touch her once more. 'Except, yet again, I underestimated the impact of our chemistry.'

Her jaw dropped, the arousal shining in her eyes urging him to lay his cards on the table.

'Even here when I must be on show, play this role that feels...borrowed, it's inescapable.' That simmer of heat in his blood he felt around her boiled over. 'That day at Nordic Care, you said we should forget our attraction. Do you still feel the same?'

'I'm certainly trying to forget it.' Colour flushed her chest and neck. 'But... I... I don't know.'

'Whereas I feel the opposite,' he admitted, a sting of disappointment in his throat. '*You* are all I can think about, even when my priority should be temporarily standing in for my father.'

Her eyes shot to his.

'I've shocked you with my own directness,' he continued, determined now to lay his feelings out. 'Would you prefer that I lie to you? That I conceal how much I want you? Deceive and manipulate you into my bed instead, as you once accused me?'

She shook her head with conviction, her stare bold on his. 'No. But—'

'Be honest with me, *sötnos*,' he urged. 'The way you've always been. Because, whatever our other differences, our bodies don't seem to care. In this—' he pointed between them, illustrating the sexual tension coiling between them like smoke '—we are absolute equals.'

She dragged in a ragged breath, as if resolved. 'I want you too.'

The sweet-sounding words left her in a rush.

'But I can't lose my job and it feels…dangerous.' Her breath came faster, her breasts rising and falling.

'I guarantee your job will be safe.' He stepped closer, taking her hand and placing it over the medals she'd admired on his chest to show his sincerity. 'You have my word—as a prince, as a Knight of Varborg and a string of other titles.'

She regarded him silently and thoughtfully for long seconds, her lip snagged under teeth. Then she rolled back her shoulders. 'No one can know.'

Andreas nodded solemnly, his pulse pounding with excitement at this negotiation of terms. 'I never again want to hurt you as I did tonight—I hate letting people down. So, tell me what you need for this to work.'

She tilted her face up so her breath brushed his lips. 'I'm not interested in relationships, so it can only be a physical thing,' she said, adding another condition of her own.

'Agreed.' Curiosity shoved a list of questions to the forefront of his mind as he inched closer, his body restless with desire. 'At present, I have more than enough to consider without…romantic complications.'

At some point in the future, he would need to

address his marital state, settle down, find a wife, produce an heir and put the needs of the principality first. But for now he could focus on pleasure and freedom—focus on Clara.

'A fling, then,' he said. Satisfaction bloomed in his chest.

'A brief fling,' she countered, her eyes swimming with need as she stared up at him.

He nodded, already forming a plan to safeguard her privacy. He didn't want his public prominence to scare her off before they'd even begun.

'I have one final condition,' he said, tugging her hand so their bodies were almost touching. 'And this one is non-negotiable, I'm afraid.'

'Oh?' A playful glint shone in her eyes. 'How very bossy of you.'

Andreas smiled. As he had that first night, he reached for a strand of her hair and eased it behind her ear, allowing his fingertips slowly to trace the curve of her cheek and down to the tip of her earlobe, where a tiny pearl earring dangled.

She shuddered and need rumbled in his chest on a stifled groan.

He stared into her eyes and rested his hand on her waist, the very air in the room seeming to crackle and hiss with electricity.

'No more curtseys. No more "Your Royal Highness",' he stated, his gaze falling to the soft excited pant of her breath over those gloss-slicked lips he wanted so badly to taste.

'It's only proper,' she said, one corner of her

mouth tugged in a knowing and defiant smile. 'After all, I *am* one of your subjects.'

His fingers curled into the fabric of her dress, an animalistic growl sounding in his head. 'Not when I'm inside you, making you come.'

Galvanised by her low moan, he hauled her close, crushing her to his chest. Their lips found the others in a rush of desperation and mutual, almost palpable, relief as they kissed. Her curves moulded to his chest and hips in all the right places, the heat of her fanning the inferno in his veins, the scent of her a dizzying cloud that made time recede. Andreas cupped the back of her head, directing her mouth, their tongues meeting and surging wildly, so nothing else seemed to matter. There was just this moment: just a man and woman; just passion and need.

Her fingers twisted in his hair, tugging, greedy to have him where she wanted him. Andreas paced forward, pressing her against the back of a sofa, his mind and body consumed by her, as he'd been since that first meeting in the guest suite when she'd effortlessly blown him away. He fisted the fabric of her dress over her hip, hoisting the dress up high enough to slide his hand around one silky bare thigh.

'Andreas,' she moaned, just as he'd hoped, dropping her head back to expose her neck to his ravaging mouth.

The sound of his name on her lips was more rewarding than anything he'd imagined. Cupping one cheek of her backside, he lifted her, depositing her bottom on the edge of the furniture so he could slot himself between her parted thighs.

He grew hard between her legs as he ran his lips over her jaw, up to her earlobe and down the silky column of her neck, sucking in her scent, filling his senses with her taste, licking and nibbling her satin-like skin. He couldn't get enough. It was as if her skin was laced with some sort of potent aphrodisiac. He'd walk away smelling of her, the scent of her torturing him for the rest of the night.

Her hands were inside his waistcoat, her touch through his shirt hot like a brand. He kissed her again, his tongue in her mouth as she dipped her hands lower to cup his buttocks, drawing his hips to hers, massaging his arousal between their bodies so Andreas almost lost his mind. This was insane. He needed to stop. But his fingers swiped the lacy edge of her underwear over her backside and sanity fled.

'Andreas...please...' she whispered, her eyes closed and her head back so her throat was exposed to him, already pink from the scrape of his facial hair and ferocity of his desire.

Her beauty was a painful throb beneath his ribs. The marks he'd left on her skin called to the primitive part of his brain, the part acting on instinct alone. If she kept calling his name in that breathy voice, he feared what he'd do next. Indulging in one last kiss, he ripped his mouth from hers, his breathing wild and painful.

'Look at me, *sötnos*,' he demanded, sliding his

fingers under the lace of her underwear to stroke the molten heat between her legs. 'Open your eyes.'

She obeyed, blinking up at him, her lips parted on a series of soft gasps as he stroked her over and over.

With his other hand, he reached for her wrist and pressed her palm over his erection, steely hard behind his fly.

'Tell me we're equals now, when I'm so hard for you it hurts and you're wet for me. Tell me. I need to hear you say it. I need to know you believe it. I don't want a puppet in my bed. I want you.'

She gripped his arm, her stare slumberous with arousal but alive with the sparks of fire that were pure Clara.

'We're equals,' she said on a ragged breath, dragging his mouth back to hers as her hips bucked against his hand.

'That's right, we are,' he murmured against her lips, against the wild kisses she snatched from him in between moans. Andreas kissed her back, the taste of triumph sweet and satisfying as he stroked her faster, sliding a finger inside her core.

'Except,' he said, rearing back to gaze into her eyes, 'I've never wanted anyone as much as I want you.'

His words seemed to tip her over the edge into bliss. She climaxed, shuddering in his arms as he kissed her through the spasms with slow thrusts of his tongue. When she was spent, she leaned her weight against him, her face buried against his neck while she caught her breath.

Andreas's heart thundered in his chest, his arm holding her tight. He slid his hand from between her legs and brushed down the hem of her dress, literally blocking out the sight of temptation. One glimpse of her naked thigh, a flash of black lace, and he might not make it back to the banquet where he was to give an after-dinner tribute to his father.

Just then, there was an insistent rap of knuckles on the door. Nils had been instructed to give him as much time as possible.

'Just a moment,' Andreas called, frustration a tight knot under his ribs.

Clara deserved more than a quick clandestine fumble. She deserved seduction and satin sheets, romance and adoration. Especially after the way he'd inadvertently hurt her over the dress. But his time with her was up. His absence at the banquet must have been noticed, and his official duties called.

'I have to get back,' he said, his hands reluctant to leave Clara's waist. He tilted up her chin and pressed a soft kiss to her lovely lips. 'I have people to schmooze, an after-dinner speech to give. Hopefully my father will be recovered from his headache and join us for the rest of the night.'

How had he completely blanked out the visiting dignitaries awaiting an audience with him as a stand-in for his father? With Clara in his arms, he'd forget his own name...

She nodded, stood and looked up at him. 'Of course. You should go.'

She was flushed from her orgasm, more beautiful than ever. She cast her eyes over him and then straightened the row of medals on his lapel, which had gone awry during their passionate tryst. 'There—perfect.'

He reached for her hand, raised it to his lips and pressed a lingering kiss over her knuckles. 'It was a pleasure negotiating with you, Ms Lund. I look forward to our next meeting, more than you could ever imagine.'

She smiled, her eyelids heavy, and his breath caught. How he wished he could whisk her away somewhere private, just the two of them.

But Clara's cold, hard reality was calling to them both. Taking once last glance at her breath-taking image, committing how she looked to memory, he tugged his jacket into place, ran a hand through his hair and left the room, pulling on his persona as he re-joined the evening's festivities.

She was right: they *were* from different worlds. Hers was less privileged, but she had greater freedom. But as long as he was careful with her feelings—as long as he never again let her down, as long as he protected her from speculation, from the royal-watchers and press critics who judged his every move—they could meet on common ground as equals.

CHAPTER EIGHT

THREE NIGHTS AFTER the banquet, Andreas was enjoying a highly erotic dream featuring his favourite nurse when he was roughly awoken by the intercom buzzer.

'Andreas, it's Clara. I need to speak to you.' The urgency of her voice shot panic through his system.

He jolted into a sitting position. 'Come in.'

He disarmed the door lock and reached for his prosthesis. His pulse bounded with surges of familiar adrenaline. He was used to being woken in the middle of the night by a pager, but never here, at home.

'What's wrong?' he asked as she appeared in his bedroom seconds later. He moved his eyes over her from head to toe. 'Are you hurt?' Why else would she come to him in the middle of the night, her voice carrying a desperate edge that made his teeth grind?

She shook her head. 'I'm concerned for Prince Henrik. I need a second opinion. It's snowing a blizzard outside, and the prince's personal physician is stuck in a snow drift.' She wrung her hands, wearing a deep frown of worry. 'I've left the prince with the other nurse on duty tonight because I wanted to be the one to wake you.'

Andreas stood and shrugged on his robe, too distracted by concern for his father to enjoy the way Clara flicked her stare over his nakedness before he tied the belt.

'You did the right thing in coming to me, *söt-nos.*' He gripped her upper arms, deeply touched that she'd sought out his help. 'I'll come right away.'

He scrubbed a hand over his face to clear the last fog of sleep and reached for the medical bag he kept on hand at all times. What could be wrong with his father?

He recalled the last conversation he'd had with the prince. His father had been a little tired, but otherwise seemed in good health. They'd talked mainly of business: the upcoming visit of the Swedish prime minister; the plans for the annual staff Christmas party; the list of new charities seeking royal patronage. But Andreas trusted Clara's clinical judgement and she wouldn't have woken him lightly.

'Tell me what your concerns are,' he said as they left the suite.

'Prince Henrik became acutely breathless a short while ago,' Clara said. 'His temperature is normal, pulse and blood pressure elevated. No history of chest pain, but obviously I'm worried about pneumonia or a pulmonary embolus, although I've listened to his chest and can't hear any evidence of consolidation.'

Concealing his own concern, Andreas placed his hand on her shoulder, squeezing for both their comfort.

'What are his oxygen saturations?' he asked as

they rushed from the guest wing towards his father's suite, fear now a metallic taste in his mouth.

'Ninety-seven,' she answered.

Andreas breathed a small sigh of relief.

'Someone has taken a motor sled to fetch the doctor,' Clara said, keeping pace with his longer strides. 'But it could take an hour. I know it's not strictly ethical for you to treat your father,' she continued as they entered the family wing of the palace, 'But I figured it was okay in such urgent and unusual circumstances.'

Andreas sent her a grateful smile, wishing he could drag her into his arms, but his father needed help. 'Thank you for taking such good care of the prince.'

There would be time later to tell her how he valued her inspiring dedication. How humbled he was that she'd come to him for advice. How privileged he felt because Clara was so fiercely independent, she demanded nothing from him.

Outside the prince's suite, Clara rested her hand on his arm. 'Andreas, are you sure you are okay to see Prince Henrik like this? He's quite distressed.'

For a second, she looked as if she might say more, but then she blinked and the moment passed.

'I appreciate your consideration of my feelings. Thank you.'

Of course she saw and understood him. Of course a nurse of her calibre would grasp the complex emotions pounding through him. Seeing a parent incapacitated was upsetting for anyone, even more so when that man was also your ruler, someone Andreas had always seen as a larger-than-life figure.

What she couldn't know was how the fear for his father chilling him to the bone was amplified by what had happened to Oscar. The last time Andreas had tried to medically help a family member, he'd failed, with devastating consequences for him, his family and the nation. He'd tried everything he could to treat and then revive his brother, but his efforts hadn't been enough.

But he couldn't think about his failings now. He needed to stay calm and objective. He rapped on the door once out of observance of royal protocol, urgency driving him to enter the suite of rooms without waiting to be admitted.

The prince's butler greeted them, the older man's face stricken and pale. 'The doctor is still thirty minutes away, Your Royal Highness. Should I call for the helicopter, sir?'

'Of course not, Møller. There's a blizzard raging outside,' Andreas said, fighting the sickening trepidation twisting his gut. 'I will assess the prince so we know what we're dealing with.'

The butler stood aside and Andreas and Clara entered his father's bedroom, a room he hadn't been in since he'd been a young boy.

No matter how hard he'd tried to prepare, given his training and Clara's words of warning, shock lashed at Andreas like the icy rain pelting the windows outside. His father was seated on the edge of the bed, another nurse at his side. He wore an oxygen mask, but his hands were braced on his thighs and his breathing was fast and laboured.

Fear and compassion tugged at Andreas's heart as he approached. 'Pappa, I need to listen to your chest.'

If he focussed on his training, treated the man before him like any other patient, he could keep the waves of panic at bay. Only this wasn't *any* patient. This was his father, his ruler, a proud and unemotional man much beloved by their nation, and something was wrong.

He reached for his father's radial pulse, noting it was elevated but regular.

'Do you have any chest pain?' His mind trawled the same differential diagnoses for acute shortness of breath that Clara had considered.

Prince Henrik shook his head, his eyes wild with distress, sweat beading on his forehead.

'Dizzy,' he gasped, gripping Andreas's hand with vice-like force.

Clara handed Andreas a stethoscope. He listened to the breath sounds, searching Clara's concerned expression for clues, because something was off. He felt as if he was the last person to know some sort of well-kept secret, his sense of isolation flaring anew. Yes, he belonged here, as Clara had pointed out, but he'd spent so long away pursuing his career that there was no one at the palace he could confide in.

Only Clara.

He focussed on the whoosh of air transmitted through the stethoscope, swallowing down his rising sense of apprehension. His father's office had given little away when it came to the 'brief illness' rendering the normally fit and active prince indisposed. But was there something more medically sinister going on than Andreas had been led to believe?

He should have pushed for more information on the prince's health when he'd returned. He didn't blame Clara, or any of the medical staff who were loyal to the prince, respectful of his privacy and duty-bound to keep his medical information confidential. But had Andreas, a doctor, failed to see something that had been right under his nose? And, if there was something serious going on, why hadn't his father confided in him?

That familiar feeling of inadequacy settled like a stone in his stomach. Would he ever be good enough in his father's eyes or would he always be the less important son? They hadn't been close for years, but they were the only family each other had left. Except now it seemed that Prince Henrik couldn't even trust his doctor son with potentially important information.

Something in Clara's stare, something she could no longer hide from him because of their growing emotional closeness, told Andreas that, unlike him, she knew the full story.

Guilt lashed him. Since his return to Varborg, he'd been self-absorbed with his struggles to reconcile the demands of his two roles, doctor and heir, because being Prince Andreas had forced him to confront his greatest failure—losing Oscar. But instinct told him this was more than a 'brief illness'. As his son and as his heir, Andreas had a right to know if his father's health was in danger.

'You're right,' he said to Clara, removing the ear-pieces of the stethoscope. 'Breath sounds are completely normal.'

He beckoned her a short distance away so they could talk. 'There's no sign of infection or acute heart failure. No obvious pneumothorax or pleural effusion. But without a chest X-ray or a scan to exclude anything more subtle but sinister our diagnostic abilities are limited.'

Clara frowned, glancing at Prince Henrik. 'So what do we do?' she whispered, looking up at him with absolute faith.

At least *she* believed in him, even if no one else did.

Remembering that he was good at his job, Andreas dragged in a shuddering breath, grateful for Clara's presence.

'I think the most likely diagnosis of exclusion is a panic attack,' he said, hoping for his father's sake that he was right, because they could easily treat that here and now. 'It's worth a shot; if we can slow down his breathing, then we'll know.'

She nodded, her expression staying impressively neutral. Andreas wasn't the prince's doctor. It wasn't Clara's place to inform him of his father's medical history. But none of that helped with his feelings of inadequacy.

Andreas sat on the bed at his father's side and

took the older man's warm and capable hand. 'Pappa, you're breathing too fast. We need to slow that down. Purse your lips like you're going to blow out a candle…that's it. Now breathe nice and slowly. In, two, three and out, two, three, four, five.'

While Andreas repeated the instructions in as calm a voice as he could muster, given the sickening, doubt-fuelled lurch of his stomach, Clara stooped in front of the prince and pursed her lips, demonstrating the slower breathing technique in time to Andreas's voice.

It took a few minutes of synchronised breathing, but eventually his father calmed, his grip on Andreas's hand reassuringly strong and unwavering, reminding Andreas of the proud statesman who'd ruled Varborg steadfastly for fifty years.

Hot with shame, he wondered how they'd ended up so estranged. The chasm between them had been so wide for so long, they knew little about each other's personal lives, fears and dreams.

'Give the prince some privacy, please.' Andreas instructed the butler and other nurse to vacate the room. 'Would you like Clara to stay so we can make you comfortable, Pappa?'

Taking some slow, shuddering breaths, his father nodded, slowly recovering his strength and composure.

Clara plumped the pillows and together they repositioned Prince Henrik back into bed.

'I think you had a panic attack, Pappa,' Andreas said, the doctor in him needing to understand why just as much as the son. 'Your physician is on his way, and I'm sure he'll organise some tests, in case we're missing something.'

'Thank you, son,' Prince Henrik said, shakily. 'That was…alarming. I'm grateful that you were here. I'm not sure what came over me.'

Andreas startled, glancing away from the man he'd looked up to his whole life. He couldn't recall a single time when Prince Henrik had relied on him emotionally. Not after Andreas's mother had died, when Prince Henrik had become focussed on Oscar as the heir, nor after the accident that had stolen the life of his eldest son. They'd grieved differently, separately, never seeing eye to eye.

'No need to thank me, Pappa. I'm always here for you. I'll stay until your doctor arrives.' He needed to understand what might have caused his father's acute distress tonight.

Clara placed a fresh glass of water next to the bed. 'Can I get you anything else, sir?'

'No, thank you, dear,' his father said with a fond smile that spoke not only of his immediate recovery, but also their close relationship. Of course Prince Henrik respected Clara. She was an exceptional nurse: gifted and smart, humble and empathetic. And, maybe most importantly, loyal.

Clara glanced at Andreas. 'I'll leave you two alone. Call if you need me.'

Her stare brimmed with empathy that filled Andreas with fresh dread. Before she could leave the room, he caught up with her, resting his hand on her arm. 'Thank you for coming to me for help,' he said, wishing he could crush her in his arms and escape into their passion. 'The prince is lucky to have you on his staff.'

'He's lucky to have *you* as a son,' she replied, her compassionate stare leaving him exposed and raw, feelings he would prefer to conceal from the woman he was trying to seduce. 'Why don't you sit with him a while, perhaps talk?'

With his throat tight with confusion and fear, Andreas nodded and re-joined his father. The alarming realisations of tonight proved that there were conversations long overdue. Seeing his father incapacitated had brought home the reality of Andreas's situation. Even if there was no sinister explanation for his father's current state of health, no one lived for ever. Like Andreas, the prince was human, as vulnerable to illness, weakness and scars, both physical and emotional, as the next man.

Prince Henrik would one day die, as was the natural order of the world, and Andreas would take his place on Varborg's throne. His days of freedom to pursue the career he loved, a career that gave him a deep sense of pride, achievement and validation, were numbered. His personal freedoms too, such as his fling with Clara. Like it or not, prepared or not, Andreas would one day need to make these sacrifices and commit fully to the role he would inherit.

It might even be sooner than he'd imagined.

CHAPTER NINE

CLARA OPENED HER EYES the next morning, disorientated after only a couple of hours' sleep. She glanced around her bedroom in the staff quarters at the palace, her first thought of Andreas.

Last night, it had been obvious that her suspicions were correct: he *was* unaware of Prince Henrik's diagnosis and terminal prognosis. She'd witnessed the moment he'd figured out something serious was going on. She'd had to look away from the pain and confusion dulling his stare, her loyalties so horribly torn between father and son.

Only now, off-duty at the palace, could she be there for Andreas. She reached for her phone and sent him a text, asking after both men. On her way to the shower, she opened the curtains. The snow drift outside the window reached halfway up the pane. There was no way her little car would make it to the main roads. It looked as if she was snowed in. She made the call to Nordic Care, informing them she wouldn't make her late shift.

Under the spray of hot water, Clara tried to process everything that had happened since the Jubilee Banquet. After they'd agreed to have a secret fling that night in the Blue Room, she'd vowed to hold herself emotionally distant, and she'd tried her best.

But the blizzard had brought about exceptional and unforeseen circumstances. Her professional reliance on him was only natural—Andreas was a geriatrician. But now, faced with the evidence that Clara knew more about the prince's medical condition than his own son, a doctor, the thrilling affair they'd negotiated seemed almost trivial.

Don't turn on me now...when I need an ally...

His heartfelt plea from the night of the banquet twisted her stomach. He had so much weight on his shoulders: the imminent loss of his father; the enforced end of his medical career; the transition to the most important role of his life, as ruler. How would he deal with all of that? How could she help him adjust?

Her phone was stubbornly silent as she dressed in her everyday clothes—jeans and a beautiful jumper hand-knitted by Alma. She'd just applied moisturiser, mascara and lip gloss and fitted her nose stud when there was a tap at the door. Expecting another of the nurses, or the staffing manager with an update on the conditions on the roads, she pulled open the door.

Andreas stood on the threshold, his eyes haunted and fatigued. He'd come to *her* of all people. Did he have no one else he trusted to talk to?

Clara's heart cracked open for him. 'I'm so sorry.'

'You know his prognosis, of course,' he said, shock etched into his haggard expression.

Even grieving, he was unbearably beautiful, dressed in a forest-green sweater and dark jeans, his hair carelessly pushed back from his face. She wanted to hold him, her protective urges on high alert. Instead, she glanced along the deserted corridor and then, when she saw that they were alone, reached for his hand.

'I'm sorry. He's my patient,' she whispered.

Andreas of all people would understand that she had a professional duty of confidentiality, but she hated that he seemed to have been the last to know.

'I'm not blaming you,' he said, flatly, 'But he's *my* father. *Someone* should have told me. *He* should have told me.'

She nodded, stunned speechless by his understandable pain and confusion.

'He trusts me to rule Varborg because he has no choice,' he continued, his voice gruff with bitterness. 'But he doesn't trust me, his heir, his son, a *doctor*, with his confidences, even when I'm the person this impacts the most.'

Of course he would hate to stop practising medicine. Sick to her stomach with wretchedness, Clara inched closer and took his other hand. 'It's a shock.'

'I should have seen the signs,' he said, briefly closing his eyes.

She wanted to be there for Andreas, but she was trapped in an impossible position of torn loyalties, already too close to this family to be totally objective.

'You can't blame yourself. And maybe *because* you're his son,' she continued cautiously, '*Because* he loves you, he's tried to spare you the distressing news.'

Andreas frowned, unconvinced.

His relationship with his father was none of her business. They weren't friends. They weren't even properly lovers. But she understood exactly what he was going through. Clara's mother had tried to spare her daughters from worry in the beginning, before she'd faced surgery and had no longer been able to hide the symptoms.

A door slammed somewhere overhead. Clara forced herself to step back. Someone might see them or overhear their conversation. They'd agreed to be discreet about their relationship.

'How *is* the prince this morning?' she asked, to cover up her caution.

'He's feeling much better, enough to refuse me the minute details of his medical records.' His voice was bitter, his expression disbelieving. 'It's as if he doesn't understand me at all. I'm a doctor; maybe I could…help.'

Clara winced in empathy. She understood his feelings of futility, but beyond supporting his father there was nothing else he could do. And she couldn't blame Prince Henrik for not wanting to rake over it all again.

'Is there anything I can do for you?' she asked. Maybe sharing her own experiences would make him feel less alone.

He looked away, clearly struggling with complex emotions. When he looked back, his stare was imploring. 'I'm…overwhelmed by it all. Powerless. I can't think straight. I need to get away from here, clear my head. Will you come?'

Clara swallowed her immediate 'yes'. She'd promised to guard her feelings, but how could she deny him a single thing when she understood his current vulnerability? Someone he loved, his *parent*, had cancer. Whereas Clara's mother had been given the all-clear, Prince Henrik had been told to put his affairs in order. And for Andreas the news carried another layer of devastation. His birth right meant he would soon have to choose: his career or the crown.

Except, he had no real choice.

'I'll go anywhere with you,' Clara said, deciding she would double her efforts to protect herself while also being there for Andreas. 'But have you seen the snow?'

'Trust me,' he said, his stare both pleading and hopeful.

'I do.' she said.

'Grab your boots,' he instructed, some of the tension leaving his body.

Clara hurried into her room to snatch them up, along with her phone.

He led her to a part of the palace she'd never visited before. There, in a large boot room, he shrugged on a fur-lined parka emblazoned with the palace crest from a selection of sizes hanging along the wall, and then passed one to Clara, along with some mittens and a hat.

Despite the sadness in the air, excitement fizzed in her veins. Would they be digging snow? Cross-country skiing? It didn't matter. He'd come to her in his hour of need. She'd do anything to help him process the news he'd received last night, including escape with him.

Outside, the snow in the courtyard had been shov-elled away and there at the top of the driveway sat a gleaming, royal-blue snow-mobile bearing the royal crest and the words House of Cronstedt.

'Can you drive that?' Clara asked, hesitating for a second as she pulled on the hat. She didn't want the heir to the throne to be injured on her watch.

Andreas smiled broadly for the first time, his eyes bright with confidence and excitement. 'Of course I can. You can't get anywhere in winter up here without one.' He took her gloved hand, lead-ing her towards the machine. 'Oscar and I used to have races.'

'Of course you did.' She laughed, picturing the scene. 'That sounds terrifying.'

'Jump on,' he said with a sexy wink that snatched her breath away.

She hadn't imagined exactly how they would implement their secret affair, but she'd guessed it would involve late-night texts and clandestine meet-ings in discreet hotels. This, on the other hand—spending time with the *real* Andreas, getting to know him better, understanding his passions and doubts—was way more dangerous to Clara.

She sat at the back. Andreas swung his leg over the seat in front and started the ignition.

'Hold tight,' he called over the hum of the engine.

Clara scooted forward to encircle his waist with her arms and his hips with her thighs so she felt the thud of his heart under her cheek. The engine revved beneath her, setting them in motion, and Clara squealed, gripping him tighter.

Then they were off, skimming the undisturbed snow which glittered in the sun like a sheet of diamonds, and headed for the native forest at the perimeter of the landscaped palace grounds. Andreas drove the snow-mobile with impressive skill, weaving them with ease over the bumpy landscape and between the tall pine trees.

The wind whipped at Clara's cheeks and hair. Her smile was so wide, her teeth were cold. This reminded her of the night of the Jubilee Banquet, when she'd danced in his arms and felt as if she were flying. The wild sense of freedom was back—the heady abandon she'd experienced far too infrequently, thanks to Lars Lund's irresponsible approach to caring for his family and raising his daughters. How many more experiences had she passed up during her teens and early twenties, time she would never get back?

She gripped Andreas's waist tighter and rested her face against his shoulder, protected from the bitter wind by the imposing breadth of his chest. Other women might get carried away by the absurd romance of this situation but Clara was weighed down by reality, even as she sped along with the sun on her back and Andreas's solid warmth seeping into her front.

Ever since they'd danced together, when she'd come alive in his arms both on the dance floor and later in the Blue Room, she'd told herself that their fling didn't make him hers. He'd said they were equals that night, when he'd forced her to admit how badly she wanted him, but deep down world-weary Clara knew better. In all the areas that mattered—their upbringings, their expectations, their priorities—they were worlds apart.

And, even if she wanted him, he belonged to Varborg first and foremost and to his future princess second. That woman would be content to walk at his side, stand in his shadow, give Varborg and him an heir and never question the inherent power imbalance of their relationship. That didn't stop Clara wanting the only thing she could allow herself—a temporary interlude in his bed, freshly stamped with an expiry date.

Finally, they emerged from the trees into a clearing. Andreas slowed the snow-mobile, bringing it to a halt and killed the engine. Clara raised her face from his shoulder and gasped with awe at the sight of a picture-perfect log cabin nestled among the fir trees with a backdrop of Varborg's northern mountain range.

'Oh… It's so beautiful,' Clara said, mesmerised. 'Who lives here?'

Like the surrounding forest, the cabin was dressed

in a thick layer of snow, glittering in the sunshine like a scene from a winter wonderland.

'No one.' Andreas held out his hand, helping her from the back of the snow-mobile with a more care-free smile on his face. 'It's a hunting lodge built by one of my Cronstedt ancestors.'

Already he seemed less tense, as if he felt more at home here than among the grandeur and cere-mony of the palace.

'Oscar and I came here all the time as boys,' he continued, confirming her suspicion. 'It was the only place we could be free to play—build bon-fires and tree houses and camp out in the summer. There's a lake over that ridge where we'd go ice-fishing in winter.'

She could envision the young prince he must have been so clearly in her mind's eye—scamper-ing around after his big brother, away from the strict protocol and public gaze of his royal life. No won-der he chose to hide out here when he needed space.

The barest flicker of pain crossed his eyes as he tugged her close. 'Now I'm the only person who spends time here.'

She blinked up at him, her heart beating wildly at the power of the cabin's solitude and the positive change already evident in Andreas.

'It's idyllic,' she said with wonder in her voice, touched that he'd brought her to this special place— a place clearly dear to him, a place linked to his fondest childhood memories of his brother.

Clara's eyes burned, close to tears for his losses.

But she *never* cried—not even when Alma Lund had haltingly confessed her cancer diagnosis to her daughters. Nor when, weeks later, nineteen-year-old Clara had swallowed her pride and called her father, begging him to come home and support his wife, the mother of his daughters, during her treatment. Of course, Lars hadn't even done it for Clara and Freja. He'd made excuses and let them down once more. She should have known better than to rely on him.

'Can we go inside?' she asked, glancing at the charming cabin, the windows of which glowed with warm, orange light, hoping to escape the humiliating rejection of that final conversation with her father.

'Of course. I asked the housekeeper to start the fires and stock the fridge.' He took her hand and led her up the steps of the covered veranda, which housed outdoor seating carved from old tree trunks and covered with reindeer pelts.

'Are you hungry?' he asked when they were inside, taking her coat and hanging it next to his on wooden pegs beside the door.

Clara stilled, overwhelmed by the sumptuous interior. The fire was roaring, warming the entire living space which boasted high-vaulted ceilings crossed with wooden beams, massive picture windows framing the views and luxurious furniture. Breakfast was laid out, the dining table romantically set for two.

She shivered, in spite of the warmth and the cosy

décor. Thinking about her father reminded her how out of her depth she was when it came to relationships. She wasn't a sophisticated seductress. After her one intimate relationship with a man who'd never called her again—proof that she'd been wasting her time with men—it had been easier to avoid disappointment than to give anyone else the power to hurt her again. And she'd been preoccupied, too busy with studying, working and helping out with her mother to devote the time to the kind of relationship *she* wanted—one on equal terms.

But Andreas wasn't just any man. She trusted him.

As if he could read the turmoil in her mind, Andreas stared down at her, his eyes dark with emotions, his expression turning serious.

'I've never brought anyone here before.' He brushed some hair from her cheek, the way he had the first night they'd kissed.

It made her feel precious. His words felt like a promise, an acknowledgement that he trusted her with his private life; that, despite his playboy past, Clara was different…for now. It sounded naïve, except she *was* different. She wasn't planning to fall in love with him, so her heart was safe. She wanted nothing from him, beyond them being equals, and perhaps more of that reckless, carefree feeling he brought out in her.

'In that case, thank you for bringing me here.' With her heart galloping, she stood on tip toes and pressed her cold lips to his warm ones, sucking in the crisp scent of snow and pine forest that seemed to cling to his skin.

She pulled back and he cupped her cheek in his palm, his earnest stare searching hers. 'No, thank *you*—for trusting me, for blindly following me, for escaping with me.'

Clara released a soft, shuddering sigh, his touch filling her body with enough heat to melt the snow outside. A part of her—a deep-seated part, home to her deepest fears—understood his need to flee reality. How many times had she experienced the same shameful urge in the middle of a long, dark night of worrying about her mother? She'd been too young to shoulder such responsibility alone, but with her father's refusal to come home there had been no one else to care for Alma.

'I wanted to tell you at the palace,' she whispered, that lost and scared part of her exposed, 'That I understand what you're going through today. My mother was diagnosed with breast cancer when I was nineteen.'

His lips flattened, his brows pinched together. 'I'm so sorry, *sötnos.*'

Clara shook her head, rushing on. 'She's fine now, but at the time there was only me and my fifteen-year-old sister to care for her. I helped out at home, drove her to her chemotherapy appointments, sat awake on her worst nights, willing her to get better.'

Clara's voice broke. Speaking about her beloved mother's illness brought those painful memories back, along with resentment at Lars for heaping too much on his daughter's shoulders. But Alma Lund had been one of the lucky ones.

'It's not the same as your situation,' she said, 'But you're not alone, Andreas. Your confusion and hurt and anger are all normal reactions.'

He cupped her face with both hands. 'Thank you for confiding that in me. That you understand, that I can talk to you, helps more than you'll ever know. Your inner strength is truly inspiring, Clara.'

'So is yours.' She couldn't seem to catch her breath, as if the air in her lungs were frozen. 'You've been through so much.'

How was she expected to keep her distance when he trusted her, had opened up to *her*, of all the people he must have in his life? But maybe he had few people with whom he felt truly understood and seen for himself. Maybe he had few people who expected nothing from him. Maybe he too was weighed down by responsibility.

'Right now, strong is the last thing I feel,' he admitted, taking her hand and holding it to his chest over the wild thump of his heart while his hungry stare traced her mouth. 'It's taking every shred of restraint I possess not to kiss you and touch you and bury myself so deep inside you that I lose myself in you, just for a few moments.'

Clara dragged in a ragged breath, recognising the same urgent needs in herself. This craving for him was building out of control. It was as if their chemistry was being fanned hotter by the fact that time was running out. Reality was chasing their tails.

Soon, when Andreas was forced to give up his career, they would no longer work together at Nordic Care. Clara's nursing position at the palace would end with Prince Henrik's death. They would have no excuse to see each other. And, while she could sleep with a prince—especially when, to her, he was simply Andreas—she couldn't sleep with Varborg's ruler, an altogether more serious and intimidating man.

'Then do it,' she said boldly, her body an inferno from the fire he'd lit inside her with that first sexy smile, when he'd been resplendent in his bath like a marauding Viking. 'It's the only thing I want from you.'

For a moment he froze, frowned, as if her words were too good to be true.

'Except,' she said, before she threw herself into his arms, 'We said we'd be equals in this. And, the thing is, I'm nowhere near as experienced as you. In fact, I've only done this once, with a guy I met at college. He pursued me, took me on romantic dates, bought me flowers, made me feel special…and then, the minute I slept with him, he lost interest. I found out he'd done that to lots of girls in my year, which was…humiliating. So I just gave up on men after that. It was easier to avoid disappointment than to risk being hurt and let down. Not to mention that it wasn't even very good and…'

His fingers landed on her lips, his eyes blazing

into hers. 'I don't care about your inexperience. It doesn't matter. That guy is an idiot.'

'It matters to *me*. I vowed that the next time I was intimate with someone it would be on equal terms and with honest expectations. That *I'd* be in control.'

He nodded, taking her seriously.

'The way you made me feel the night of the banquet,' she ploughed on, 'Alive, joyous, powerful. I've never experienced that with anyone else. I want to make you feel the same way.'

This complex, hurting man standing before her was everything; the sight, scent and feel of him filled her senses, making her feel alive again. She wanted to rock his world. She wanted to help him lose himself. They could escape the sometimes cold, harsh and cruel reality of life together.

'So, will you show me what you like?' she finished.

His pupils dilated, his jaw flexing as he took a pained-looking swallow. With a growl that Clara felt resonate throughout every inch of her body, Andreas hauled her close, crushing her mouth to his.

For a few moments, she lost herself in the fiery passion of their kiss. Andreas made it easy, holding her so tight her feet barely touched the floor; kissing her with such domination she forgot to breathe and turned dizzy; pressing her so close, she wasn't sure where her body ended and his began.

'You might kill me...' He groaned against her

lips, pulling back to stare hard into her eyes. 'Just when I thought you couldn't be more perfect.'

Clara snorted, almost euphoric with desire. 'I'm very far from that. And I'm certain killing the heir to the throne *is* a punishable offence.'

'Then,' he said, cupping her face and kissing her once more, 'It's a good thing that right now, with you, I'm just Andreas.'

Then he took her hand and led her through the lodge to the master bedroom.

CHAPTER TEN

CLARA GLANCED AROUND the luxurious room, her body burning with need. Fur pelts covered the hardwood floor in front of the fire, which crackled and flickered, casting a warm glow. A massive carved timber bed covered with snowy white linen dominated the room.

She spun to face Andreas, reached up on tip toes and pressed her lips to his, blocking her mind to everything but the way he made her feel. She didn't want to think about the risks she was taking by allowing him this close, or reality awaiting them beyond this room. She just wanted the promise they'd negotiated: the two of them together, just a man and a woman as equals.

'I want you,' she said, slipping her hands under his jumper, seeking out his warm, golden skin, tracing every dip and bulge of the muscles she remembered from the bath. Impatient, she broke free of his kiss and pushed up his sweater so she could see his magnificent body once more, confirmation that, in this moment, he was real and he was hers.

'There's no rush,' he said, tugging his sweater over his head and tossing it to the chair beside the bed before dragging her into his arms, where the heat of him nearly burned her alive.

'I can't help myself.' She sighed. 'I've seen you naked, don't forget—*twice*.'

Clara moved her stare over the breadth of his bare chest, her hands skimming warm flesh as she went. He was beautiful, so masculine the woman in her trembled with longing for the empowering connection they shared.

'I thought I caught you checking me out last night.' A satisfied smiled kicked up his mouth. He raised her chin, his breath whispering over her lips. 'So it's only fair if I now feast my eyes on every inch of this body that has tortured me night and day since we met.'

His warm hands slid under her jumper, deftly freeing the clasp of her bra with one flick of his fingers. He kissed her in a long and thorough exploration that left her shifting restlessly against him to appease the molten ache between her legs.

How had this man, unlike any other, inspired such desperate need? Was it just the way he looked at her, the way he'd always looked at her, as if to him she was…exceptional and unique? Had she spent too long shutting down this side of herself, so one look at him had sent her hormones into revolt?

They reached for the hem of her sweater in unison, Andreas removing both it and her bra in one swift move so she shivered before him, not with nerves but with delicious anticipation. Goose pimples rose on her skin, but she was burning up. Chest to chest with Andreas, naked skin to naked skin, she felt as if she might incinerate to ash.

'Touch me,' she begged when he only stared at her nakedness.

His eyes blazed as he raised his hands to caress her bare breasts. 'You are breathtakingly beautiful.' His voice was gruff with desire.

Clara gasped but it wasn't enough. It was nowhere near enough for that reckless part of her that craved the life-affirming freedom of his touch.

'I wanted you that first time I saw you,' he said, his thumbs toying her nipples to taut peaks. 'With your hair all prim and proper and your uniform fuelling some pretty raunchy nurse fantasies I never knew I had.'

Clara laughed and bit down on her lower lip to try and contain the swell of pleasure weakening her legs, but languid heat radiated out from his expert touch, infecting her entire body.

'I wanted you too,' she said, dropping her head back so her throat was exposed to his kisses. 'You looked so rugged and wild; I was tempted to join you in that giant bath.'

Her hands roamed his shoulders, his back and arms, the sheer strength of him. She couldn't seem to touch him enough.

'I knew it would be like this between us,' he said, pressing her erect nipples between his fingers so darts of pleasure arced to her pelvis. 'I felt the sparks the first time you looked at me as if you wanted to roll your eyes, as if you didn't care *who* I was.'

Clara moaned at his words and the pleasure he

was wreaking with just his fingers and thumbs. She was already lost, whereas he seemed far too in control. Raising on tip toes to kiss him, she slid one hand down his body, his skin scalding her palm until she reached the impressive hard length of him pressing at the front of his jeans. He groaned into their kiss, gripping her tighter so she was crushed against the fiery heat of him, enclosed in his powerful arms.

But she felt powerful too, the knowledge that she could affect him as much as he affected her almost as drugging as his heated kisses.

He walked her back towards the bed. 'Lie back,' he ordered, as her thighs hit the edge of the bed. 'I want to see all of you.'

Leaning over her, he pressed kisses over her neck and chest, taking one nipple into his mouth and sucking until Clara's head spun with thick, paralysing desire. Why had she never prioritised this exploration of passion before? Surely she'd been denying herself something as essential as breathing? But would it be like this with anyone else? Her one fumbling foray into sex had been underwhelmingly brief and disappointing.

Perhaps this magic was down to Andreas. Because she'd yet to render him anywhere near as helpless as he was making her, she reached for the fly of his jeans.

His hips jerked and he took her hand, pinning her wrist to the bed. 'I believe there is a nudity imbalance to redress,' he said, smiling wickedly as he captured the other nipple with his lips, laving it with the flat of his tongue. 'You've seen me naked twice, after all.'

'Andreas...' Clara moaned, writhing beneath him on the bed as he continued to torture her breasts with the sensual pleasure of his mouth. She wasn't even naked and he'd driven her so close to the edge.

'Keep calling me that, *sötnos*,' he ordered, keeping his mouth on her breast.

He undid her jeans and together they shimmied them off with increasingly frantic tugs and shoves. Clara wanted him naked again, his weight on top of her, the heat of him scalding her, the feel of him inside her.

'Almost good enough,' he said, leaning back to move his eyes over her body from head to toe. 'But not quite perfect.'

Taking hold of her underwear, he peeled it off so slowly, so intently, with his stare scouring her nudity, Clara thought she might explode from longing.

'Don't mind me,' she whispered, her voice hoarse with want even as she tried to lighten the moment with humour. 'Have a good look.'

Andreas's eyes blazed in the firelight, showing her that he recalled the reference from the first night they'd met when *he'd* been the naked one and she'd ogled him shamelessly.

'Oh, I will, don't worry. You asked me to show you what I like and it's this—you. I intend to see and kiss and pleasure every inch of you until you sob my name. Until you never think to call me anything else but Andreas. Until to you I'm just the man who wants you so badly, he's struggling to draw breath right now.'

Everything in Clara clenched hard. How was she supposed to stay immune when he said things like that? When he looked down at her as if she was something rare, to be valued? When he made her feel as if this connection of theirs was as important to him as it was to her?

True to his word, he kissed a path across her ribs, to her belly button and lower. Clara gasped as he covered her sex with his mouth, sending fiery darts of pleasure through her every nerve. Reflexively, her fingers speared through his hair and she held on tight, her body tossed from pleasure to ecstasy to want in a cycle that happened again and again, until she was certain there was nowhere left to climb. Until she was indeed sobbing his name, as he wanted. Until she burned in white-hot fire.

Then he stopped. 'I want to be inside you when you come.' He reared back to remove his jeans and underwear so his erection sprang free, prouder and impossibly bigger than the last time she'd seen him aroused.

Aware that, for all her talk of equality and control she'd yet to do one thing to turn him on, Clara sat up and reached for him, encircling his hard length with her hand, then leaning forward to kiss him in return.

'Clara…' Andreas groaned, his stare fierce on

hers as his fingers slid through her hair, holding her to him.

'Don't you like it?' she asked, stroking the silky soft and steely hardness of him with her fingers, thumb and the tip of her tongue.

'I like it too much.' He hissed through his teeth as she took him inside her mouth, his stare glitteringly hard while he cupped her face and watched.

She'd barely taken two or three swipes of him with her tongue when he yanked her away and pulled open the bedside drawer for a condom.

'I was enjoying myself,' Clara said, pouting as he tore into the condom and stretched it on.

'So was I.' Following her down onto the bed, Andreas removed his prosthesis and tossed it to the floor.

'Come here,' he said, reaching for her, his strong arms rolling her on top. 'I love the smell of your hair,' he said as it fell around them like two curtains. 'Like spring meadows.'

Gripping the back of her neck, he dragged her lips down to his, groaning when she pushed her tongue into his mouth, the way she'd licked him seconds ago. He cupped her buttocks in his hands where she sat astride his hips, pressing her close so her sensitised core met his hard length and stars danced behind her eyes as she forgot to breathe.

'Andreas,' she pleaded, looking down at him while he commanded her hips to a torturous rhythm, up and down, over and over, sliding them together so they gasped in unison. Then, with a deft and speedy roll, he switched their positions so that he was now on top, his expression harsh with desire. Cupping her breast, he sucked the nipple to a hard peak.

'You make me so hard,' he said, his thumb rubbing the sensitive nipple he'd primed with his mouth as he watched her pleasured cries.

'I want to make you feel good,' she said, feeling him between her legs, nudging at her entrance so she spread her legs wider in invitation. 'I want you to lose yourself.'

He brushed her lips with his in a series of slow, sensual kisses. 'I like who I am when I'm with you. I like how you see me. How you're not afraid to challenge me. You make me feel as if I can be myself.'

'You can,' Clara whispered, watching arousal and vulnerability cross his beautiful stare, certain that this moment couldn't be any more perfect. Then he pushed inside her, inch by inch, until they were one.

Every muscle in Andreas's body pulled taut as though he might explode and cease to exist. Clara gasped her pleasure against his lips, staring up at him as if he was the answer to prayers, she hadn't even known she had.

Holding himself still because she felt too good, he kissed her with languid swipes of his tongue against hers, coaxing out her moans, his whispered name, her pleading expression.

But still he held them both suspended. A connection like theirs deserved savouring. If he could have kept her here indefinitely in his favourite place, he would have, slaking his uncontrollable hunger for her over and over until his world made crystal-clear sense. Until he'd garnered the strength to face everything he must.

'Thank you for escaping with me,' he said, entwining his fingers through hers as he slowly thrust inside her.

He wanted to pleasure her to the point of exhaustion. His selfish need for her shocked him. She gave so much of herself, met him fearlessly, even in moments when their differences outweighed their similarities. And he couldn't seem to get enough.

'I'm so glad I met you.' He reared back and stared into her intensely vulnerable eyes, wondering how, when she'd claimed to being the less experienced, he'd ended up feeling so moved, humbled and entranced by her responsiveness and her honest passion.

'Don't stop,' she pleaded, her hands in his hair, stroking his shoulders, his back, her nails a gentle scrape that made every nerve in his body sing. It was taking every scrap of self-control he possessed not to rush to the finish. But he'd exhaust himself to make this good for her, after she'd not only trusted him with her body and her pleasure but had also opened herself to him emotionally, telling him about her mother and had been there for him when he'd needed her most.

'You're amazing,' he said, refusing to think what he'd have done if she hadn't been snowed in at the palace. He'd known it from the start when she'd strode into his bathroom and jolted his world off its axis. Shifting his weight, he rocked his hips, watching her arousal streak across her beautiful face, the flames between them fanning higher.

'Andreas!' she cried, her stare clinging to his, giving him everything he could possibly need: connection; acceptance; unity. But that was Clara: fiercely loyal; inspiringly compassionate; unflinchingly brave. He moved inside her, his kisses as wild as the beat of his heart. Every part of him coalesced, mind, body and soul, to this one moment where he truly was lost in Clara.

'Andreas… Andreas,' she said his name, calling to that inner part of him that, for some reason, with her had always found peace. Maybe because she took him at face value. Because, as she'd said, she wanted nothing from him but this.

Because he didn't want to think about tomorrow, or how long they'd have to enjoy each other as lovers, he drove himself harder. 'Lose yourself with me, Clara,' he groaned against her neck, sweat breaking out and slicking their bodies even closer together.

Temperatures soared. Hearts thudded. Stares were locked and vulnerable.

Another cry was snatched from her throat. He dived to swallow it up, thrusting his tongue into her mouth as she climaxed, her nails digging into his back, her muffled sobs sweet music to his ears.

She was his—perfection.

He followed her, the powerful spasms of his orgasm endlessly racking his body as they clung to each other, panting and sweaty and equally laid bare.

'I didn't know it could be like that,' she said breathlessly a few minutes later, wonder in her voice. 'I've heard the myths, read it in romance novels, but... wow.'

'Wow indeed, *sötnos*,' Andreas said, pressing kisses to her smiling lips, her flushed cheeks, her closed eyelids while his heart fought to get back inside his chest. 'It's not always like that, but I'd say that definitely makes us equals.'

He rolled over, scooping an arm around her shoulders to hold her close while his awareness sharpened at the periphery, the intrusion of reality returning. He clung to Clara, clung to her uncomplicated company and the relentless attraction that had helped him to escape his troubles for a while.

But he couldn't escape with Clara for ever. He couldn't even stay at the lodge with her indefinitely, no matter how sorely he was tempted. He'd have to return to the palace and be there for his father, plan an exit strategy for his career.

His throat tightened with grief—for his father, the man, the ruler; the only family Andreas had left. And for himself: for that part of him that was proud of what he'd achieved; for the loss of the life he'd assumed he'd have for many years to come; for the demise of his freedom.

Clara rested her head on his chest, her hand stroking his abdomen in a way that would soon make him hard again. Andreas focussed on breathing, on the feel of her body against his, of the scent of her all over his skin. Considering today had begun with the devastating news of his father's diagnosis—and the bitter taste of failure that he'd not only missed the signs, but had also been the last person to know— that he could feel anything like the kind of pleasure and contentment that had just ripped through him was a testament to how badly he wanted this woman. Right now, she was the only thing keeping him grounded.

Except he'd also have to sacrifice even Clara.

'Do you think your Cronstedt ancestor, the one who built this place, brought his mistress here?' she asked sleepily, her lips pressing against his chest.

'Prince Erno, my great-great-grandfather? Probably. He did have a mistress, a famously beautiful one.' Had Erno Cronstedt sought solace from the demands of his position in the arms of a woman? 'Except, you're not my mistress.'

'No,' she stated simply, leaning up on her hand to peer down at him curiously, a small smile on her lips.

'I should be so lucky,' he said, stealing a kiss, because she was too far away and he already ached for her again.

Clara laughed, glancing at the fire in the hearth. 'It's dying down; I'll throw on another couple of logs.'

Before he could stop her, she slid from the bed

and crossed the room, completely naked and completely comfortable.

Andreas folded one arm behind his head, propping himself up for a better view, his mouth dry with lust and longing. How could she do that to him, turn him on and make him ravenous, within minutes of great sex? Was it some sort of power she had over him? Or was it that their connection was deeper because they worked together and because Clara also cared for his dying father? Because she saw him like no other and understood his feelings?

Every other thought in his head evaporated as she stooped and placed two more logs on the embers and then returned to the bedside, her stunning naked body cast with an orange glow from the fire.

'If this hadn't already been my favourite place in the whole world,' he said, his voice gruff with thick desire, 'It would definitely be now. I'll never be able to look at that fire again without seeing your glorious body.'

She smiled. 'I am your eternal servant, Your Royal Highness.' She gave a mock curtsey and then joined him under the sheets.

'Don't,' he said, clasping her chin, directing her mouth to his. 'We made a deal: no more curtseys.'

He kissed her, pushing his tongue against hers to try and calm the wild need uncurling in him once more. But her careless reminder had broken the spell. No matter how good it had felt to flee the palace with Clara, no matter how thoroughly he'd lost himself inside the warm haven of her body, he couldn't hide for ever from his life, his responsibilities and the difficult days ahead.

Prince Henrik needed him—the nation, too. But could he bear to lose everything in one fell swoop: his father, his career *and* Clara?

'I'm sorry,' she whispered, the playfulness draining from her eyes. 'It's too soon to joke about that, right?'

Andreas sighed, reaching for her and sliding her body under his so their rapid heartbeats aligned. 'I would normally have a sense of humour. It's just that this is the one place I've always felt I can be myself.'

He touched the glinting green gemstone in her nose, one of many facets that made Clara unique. 'And I want to be myself with you. Always.'

She nodded, regarding him thoughtfully, her stare filled with compassion when he'd rather see it burn with desire. How could she make him feel more naked than he'd ever felt in his life? He was supposed to be the one in control of this rampant attraction, he was supposed to be the one with more experience, but instead he was close to unravelling, his need for her unstoppable.

'I'm glad that you have somewhere you feel safe and free.' Her stare flicked between his eyes, as if she saw him deep to the centre of his damaged soul. 'You feel close to Oscar here too, don't you?'

He pressed a kiss to her lips. 'You have a gift for seeing people clearly, did you know that?'

He'd always appreciated her directness. But now that he'd faced the reality his father was terminal—

now that he'd escaped with Clara to this magical and unique place; now that they'd finally surrendered to their desires—his past mistakes were the last thing he wanted to discuss.

Except Clara had been there for him this morning when he'd needed someone like he'd never needed anyone before. She understood what he was going through because of her experiences with her mother. His world was on its head, the sands of time slipping through his fingers, and no amount of holding on would slow the inevitable. Discovering his father's prognosis had changed *everything*.

'I do feel close to Oscar here,' he said with a small sigh of surrender. 'We had the best times growing up.'

'You must miss him terribly,' she whispered, her fingers stroking his back hypnotically.

Andreas watched Clara's parted lips, craving a distraction from the shame, guilt and pain of re-membering. It would be so easy to kiss her again, to refocus on their passion, to seduce her into silence and get lost once more. But his recent experience with his father had taught him that he couldn't hide from his feelings for ever. They caught up with him one way or another, often when he was most vul-nerable and least expecting it.

'We were so close as boys,' he said. 'Not so much as teens, but then close again as adults before he died.'

He rolled onto his back, tucking Clara against his side so he could stare blindly at the ceiling. He didn't want to see her reaction if he had to talk about this. He wanted her to look at him with arousal, need and desperation, not pity and blame.

'Lots of siblings drift apart as teenagers,' she said, resting her cheek on his chest. 'My sister and I used to fight all the time.'

'Now, why is that so easy to imagine?' he teased, stealing another kiss for strength. 'The truth is, I hero-worshipped Oscar. He was smart and funny and always won the snow-mobile races.'

Clara smiled indulgently, her eyes bright with empathy. 'What happened to change that?'

'Nothing *he* did.' Andreas stroked his fingers up and down her back, from her nape to the top of her buttocks, her warm, silky skin comforting even as he stepped out of the shameful shadows and into the harsh light. Would she change towards him once she knew all the ugliness of his past? Could he bear that now that he'd found something real with her?

'I was fourteen and Oscar was sixteen when our mother died,' he said, because she'd always been easy to confide in. 'It seemed that, overnight, we stopped doing everything together. Oscar was suddenly too busy for races. He was always squirrelled away in Pappa's study or attending statesman classes or meeting with important dignitaries.'

'And you felt left out,' she whispered. 'That's understandable.'

Her statement jabbed at his ribs like a blow, the emotions too complex for a simple yes or no answer. He clenched his jaw, debating whether to share more. He didn't want her to see him this way—hung up on the past, a man who'd failed and let down his loved ones, at odds with his dying father.

He craved the way she'd looked at him in the bath that first day; the way she'd looked at him as he'd twirled her around the ballroom; the way she'd looked at him when she'd asked him to show her his desires.

'I didn't understand it fully at the time,' he continued, the inexplicable urge to be honest burning in his throat. 'But of course Oscar was in training to rule. I didn't blame him, after all; it was his birth right. But I was a kid, and a relatively sheltered one at that. There was a part of me that couldn't help but vie for a little of our father's attention.'

'Of course not. You were grieving for your mother. A part of you must have felt as if you'd lost your father and brother too,' Clara said simply, pressing her lips to his chest so he felt raw inside.

Was that true? It seemed obvious now.

Andreas stared hard into her eyes, as if he could draw on Clara's innate strength and intuition. 'After a while I gave up that fight. Oscar was focussed on the role he'd been born for and Prince Henrik threw himself into preparing his heir.'

'Perhaps your father was grieving too,' she said quietly.

'Perhaps. For a while, I acted out, frequented wild parties, saw the sense of freedom as a green light for anything I chose to do.'

'I've seen the pictures on the Internet.' Clara smiled sadly in understanding.

He nodded. 'Then I got wise and realised that, while I might not be as important as Oscar, I had freedom. I could choose how to fill my time and live my life. So I knuckled down, went to university, earned a medical degree and then joined the armed forces.'

'You are just as important as the next person,' she said, pushing up onto her elbows, her stare glittering with sincerity. 'Even if you'd chosen to simply be that playboy version of yourself and nothing more.'

Andreas hauled her closer and kissed her again, part of him splintering apart that she understood his motivations when he'd been blind to them, perhaps until this very second. 'And you are wise beyond your years, Nurse Lund.'

'We both had to grow up fast,' she said, her insight slicing through him like a blade.

He'd never thought of it that way, but of course losing his mother and effectively losing his brother and father to more important duties had left his teenage self lonely and confused. No wonder he'd acted out. No wonder he'd pushed himself into a medical career he could be proud of, as if he'd had something to prove to the father and older brother he loved.

And it had worked—right up to the moment when he'd been unable to save Oscar.

'And now you must soon give up all of your hard

work,' she said hesitantly. 'It must be difficult. I can't imagine ever giving up nursing.'

Something rumbled in his chest, an unsettled gnaw of uncertainty, as if her statement was another blow to the convictions that had seen him through his adult life to date. But of course Clara fiercely valued her independence, another of her attractive qualities.

'I've always known that my family must come first,' he said, dejected because, whereas Clara could continue with her career, he would be taking another path. Their worlds, the common ground they'd shared as medical colleagues, would diverge.

He continued, refusing to think about him and Clara parting ways. 'But naïvely I never truly thought about what it would mean for the career I love and take pride in until the accident that killed Oscar. I was there when he died. I tried to save him. That's how I lost my leg.'

And now, with his father's news, he had even less time left as a doctor than he'd hoped. He would have to step into Oscar's shoes, final confirmation that his brother was gone for ever...

'I'm so sorry.' She pressed her lips to his neck.

'The palace wanted me to give up medicine immediately after Oscar's funeral,' he said, recalling the rows that had driven the wedge deeper between he and his father. 'I woke up in hospital to discover my brother hadn't made it, that my leg had to be amputated; that I had to set all of that aside, put on my uniform and attend his televised state funeral. I refused to even consider giving up my career on top of everything else. And I'm glad I didn't succumb to pressure. I needed to heal and recover. I needed a reason to strap on that prosthesis every day, to do my exercises, to learn to walk again. In a way, the drive to get back to work saved me.'

Clara stroked her fingers through his hair. 'A strong motivation to recover helps. It must have been a horrendous time for you.'

'Of course, now I'm going to lose my father too. None of our past issues matter.'

He swallowed, the sense of failure intensifying. 'Not our mutual stubbornness that used to drive my mother mad, or our differences of opinion on how to rule the principality or our inability to even discuss what happened to Oscar—none of it matters.'

Defeated, he clamped his lips together, sickened by his pity party. Giving up his career, while regrettable, wasn't the end of the world. He'd adapt; he'd adapted before, to losing a limb. He could pour all his energy into his royal role. He'd do it for Oscar and try to be as good a ruler as his brother would have been.

'I'm so sorry, Andreas.' Clara wrapped her arms around his shoulders and held him tight. 'But I think you're wrong. I think that stuff with your father *does* matter. You have an opportunity not many people get, to talk about the things that have impacted your relationship before it's too late.'

Andreas stiffened. 'The men of this family don't really talk about their feelings. It's an unspoken rule to suck it up and get on with it. Even when Prince Henrik told me his diagnosis, he showed no emotion, and when I pressed for more information he as good as told me to mind my own business.'

He didn't need verbal confirmation from Prince Henrik that, as the second son, he wasn't the heir his father had hoped for. He carried enough self-doubt. If he messed up as heir, he'd not only be letting down his father and the nation, he'd also be failing the brother he hadn't been able to save in life.

'I appreciate your opinion.' He tried to keep his voice even. 'But some things are best left alone. My father is a proud man who's used to being in charge. He won't tolerate being questioned, and I've no desire to upset him during whatever time he has left. And besides, every time we do speak on an emotive subject, a part of me seems to revert to being that young boy so eager for his approval.'

He was done with that.

'We have a complex relationship, *sötnos*.' He pressed a kiss to her forehead to lessen the sting of his words, part of him regretting that he'd opened himself up quite so much.

'Don't do that.' She pulled away, drawing the sheet higher to cover her breasts. 'Don't patronise me. I know all about complex parental relationships.'

'I didn't mean to upset you,' he said, contrite. 'Will you tell me about it?'

Her frown deepened, pain in her eyes. 'By the time my father left us—I was sixteen—he'd already let me down one time too many. For three years I survived without him. Yes, I worked hard to help out Mum, but we were happier somehow, just the three of us. When my mother got sick, I was so scared. One day, I swallowed my pride and called him. I begged him to come home and help care for his wife and to support Freja, who was only fifteen. Do you know what he did? He made excuses, dismissed my concerns, said he'd try, but he had a big deal on the horizon. It was so humiliating. Before I'd even hung up the phone I knew he wouldn't come back. He didn't care about any of us. He chose his own selfish pursuits over his wife and daughters.'

'I'm sorry.' How he wished he could brush away her sadness and wished he'd been more careful with his words, or simply seduced her again rather than talking.

'I got smart—got on with my life,' she continued as if he hadn't interrupted. 'I never relied on him again, never needed him. I stopped presenting myself for his rejection.'

She turned to face him. 'But, by cutting myself off, I never had the chance to tell him how badly he'd let me down, how much he'd hurt me…and I never had the opportunity to work through forgiving him. He died two years ago. I hadn't seen him or spoken to him since that last phone call.'

He took her hand and raised it to his lips, lingering over the kiss he placed on her knuckles to show her the depth of his regret. 'If you could confront him today, what would you say?'

Clara raised her chin. 'That I no longer need him for anything. That he can't hurt or disappoint me any more. That I'm sorry he couldn't be a better man.'

Andreas's heart ached for this beautiful woman who gave so much of herself to others and somehow, intuitively, saw what they needed. His protective urges flared. He wanted to take care of her, to give her as much as she'd given him. To protect her from ever again feeling that degree of hurt and disappointment. But, of course, he *would* react that way to a wonderful woman he was not only sleeping with, but working with while she cared for his terminally ill father. Their lives were repeatedly entwined.

'I think you're wrong, too, *sötnos*,' he said. 'A while ago, you said we're from different worlds, but I think we're more similar than either of us realise.'

They'd faced similar emotional issues, dealing with them differently.

'Maybe,' she said, kissing him so he started to lose track of his thoughts. 'And maybe we should be doing other things than talking before we have to go back to reality.'

Relief washed over him as they retreated to their passion. 'I like the way you think.' In fact, he liked everything about Clara—*everything*. He rolled her underneath him, pressing his lips to hers to block out the doubts and the pain, the past and the future.

But her confessions tumbled through his mind. Bringing her here, to a place he cherished, he felt closer to her than ever. Hearing how badly she'd been hurt by her father, he vowed to take special care of her until he had to give her up.

Because he never wanted to be the one to let her down.

CHAPTER ELEVEN

A WEEK LATER, Clara was working a shift at Nordic Care, well and truly thrust back into reality. She checked the vital signs of her frail, elderly patient, Mrs Kaase, noting her most recent blood pressure on the chart. Needing a second opinion on the case, she'd summoned the registrar for advice.

Despite speaking to Andreas daily, she hadn't seen him since that magical day at the hunting lodge. They'd worked opposite shifts at the hospital, and whenever she'd worked at the palace he'd been busy with his increasing workload of royal engagements. He'd been furious over a leak to the press on the state of Prince Henrik's health, warning Clara that the palace had been forced to issue a public statement announcing his diagnosis. The story, complete with a video clip of Andreas arriving at a prominent children's charity for which he was patron, flooded the media.

Clara had watched it a hundred times just to see a glimpse of his dazzling smile. But watching his life unfold from afar, like the rest of the nation, made him seem so untouchable, they might as well have been strangers again. The absence of him served as a timely reminder: no matter how close she felt to Varborg's heir, he didn't belong to her.

Just then, the door to Mrs Kaase's room opened. Clara looked up, expecting the new registrar, Dr Nilsen.

But it was Andreas.

Their eyes met. Clara's skin tingled, as if imprinted with his every touch. If she'd known he was working today, she'd have applied mascara and the perfume he liked. Before she could fully register the heat and hunger in his stare, she realised he wasn't alone. Sister stood possessively at his side, casting Clara a disapproving look.

Clara forced her expression into something appropriate. 'I called Dr Nilsen.'

Ignoring her body's instant response to the sight of Andreas, she glanced nervously at Sister.

'Dr Cronstedt is very busy, Nurse,' Sister said, as if protecting him from predatory females. 'There's a film crew arriving soon to interview him.'

'Yes, thank you, Sister,' Andreas interjected. 'I have plenty of time to review Nurse Lund's patient.' He held Clara's stare, as if conveying a secret message with his eyes. 'I'm not supposed to be working today, but I was missing my favourite nurses here at Nordic Care.'

He winked at Sister, who flushed with delight. When he looked back at Clara, his expression innocent, his sinful lips twitched.

She swallowed, lightheaded with lust. She recalled the feel of those lips against every inch of her skin, especially between her legs. Disgusted by her weakness for him, she looked away. One day in his bed, and she was ready to forget her professionalism and hurl herself at him at work. But her need for him was a choice, not a necessity. She could kick the habit any time.

'So, what's bothering you, Clara?' He glanced at sleeping Mrs Kaase and stepped closer, reaching for her chart.

Desperation to touch him curled tightly inside Clara like an over-wound spring. Okay, maybe for now she was hooked, but just because he'd taught her that sex could be phenomenal when it was with the right person didn't mean she should act all starry-eyed. Even if they'd been alone, they had work to do.

'I'm concerned about Mrs Kaase's increasing breathlessness,' Clara said, conscious that Andreas most likely had a hundred other things to do rather than investigate her clinical hunch.

'Is that all?' Sister asked. 'Maybe you should have run this past me before calling the doctor.'

'I'm here now, Sister.' Andreas said, staring at Clara encouragingly. 'Go on.'

His observation lit her up as if she were made of electric currents, every one of them connected to the pleasure centres in her brain. But on closer inspection there was a tightness around his mouth, fatigue in his eyes. He seemed…distracted. He had so much going on. *She* was the least of his priorities, and that was fine with her.

Except this was about their patient. 'She's seven

days' post-right ventricular myocardial infarction,' she continued, undaunted.

'So you're thinking right heart failure?' he asked, his confidence in her clinical acumen obvious from the impressed approval shining in his eyes. Most doctors wouldn't have asked for her opinion.

'Yes...' she said, hating the hesitation in her voice.

She shouldn't doubt herself or her powers of observation and critical thinking just because they'd slept together. Was it just the presence of the sour-faced sister, who assumed Andreas the heir was too busy to care about his patients, when Clara knew better because she knew *him*? Or was it the things they'd shared about their respective fathers? He'd pretty quickly shut down her suggestion that he speak to Prince Henrik, letting her know when she'd crossed the line, and she'd had to pull him up on his thoughtless assumption that he was the only one with a complex father-child relationship.

But Clara didn't need his approval to do her job.

'She has worsening peripheral oedema and weight gain,' she continued, pressing home her argument. 'She's also complaining of non-specific abdominal pain.'

'I agree. It sounds like right-sided failure,' he said. 'Let's examine Mrs Kaase.'

He gently placed a hand on the patient's shoulder to wake her. 'Mrs Kaase, I need to have a listen to your heart and lungs, okay?'

The patient nodded sleepily, and Clara helped her into a sitting position. With his auscultation complete, Andreas looped his stethoscope around his neck and palpated the patient's abdomen, encouraging Clara to do the same, particularly focussing on the right-upper quadrant, where she felt an unmistakeable liver edge that indicated hepatomegaly.

'The jugular venous pressure is elevated,' he said to Clara, indicating the distended vein in the woman's neck. 'I'll site a central line to monitor the central venous pressure and order an echo.'

He addressed the patient. 'Nurse Lund and I are a little concerned that your heart isn't pumping very effectively.'

The elderly lady reached for his hand. Andreas wrapped his large, capable hands around Mrs Kaase's frail one and something in Clara's chest jolted. The medical profession would lose a great doctor when Varborg's heir became ruler. But the hospital's loss would be the nation's gain. Just like the older brother he admired so much, Andreas would excel at anything.

If only he could resolve his issues with Prince Henrik. If only he'd talk to the man before it was too late. If he fully embraced the role that was his by birth, rather than seeing himself second choice, he'd not only be good, he'd be incredible.

Her stomach swooped with the realisation that soon they'd no longer be working together. It shouldn't bother her, but maybe she was getting too close. Maybe that was why she was so invested in his happiness, why his praise and collaboration affected her so deeply... But she couldn't become reliant on him.

'I'll speak to the High Dependency Unit and organise her transfer,' he said. 'Is she on diuretics?'

Clara nodded, handing him Mrs Kaase's drug chart. 'I'll set up a central line tray.'

Grateful to escape for a moment, she left Andreas to explain the minimally invasive procedure to the patient, while she collected the portable ultrasound machine and the equipment he would need to site the central venous catheter. Her hands trembled as she gathered wrapped sterile syringes and dressings. Just because professionally and intimately Andreas treated her as his equal didn't mean she should forget her hard-won autonomy. If she wasn't careful, if she confused amazing sex and professional camaraderie for other feelings, she could so easily be hurt, given her lack of experience with relationships.

Feelings made a person vulnerable. She'd seen that in her parents' marriage; had seen her mother's tendency to forgive her neglectful husband again and again in the name of love. Clara had no intention of falling into the same trap.

Assisted by Clara, Andreas skilfully sited the central line in the internal jugular vein in Mrs Kaase's neck before accompanying Clara and the patient to the HDU. After handing over their patient, they left the ward together, an awkward silence descending.

'I've missed you,' he said finally.

The stark need, heat and restraint in his eyes all but sent Clara bursting into flames. Gone was the dedicated doctor and the regal prince. In his place stood the stripped-back man—a complex and flawed man she now knew intimately. But she needed to be careful.

'Me too,' she whispered, her entire body molten-hot.

His eyes sparked with triumph, his sexy mouth tugged in a knowing smile. Despite her warnings to herself, she ached for him. She'd do almost anything to feel his lips on her skin, to hear him groan her name, to feel him fill that empty place deep in her core. But this physical dependency to him was linked to Andreas's skills as a lover. It certainly didn't mean that she was *emotionally* dependent.

'Come to me—tonight.' It was an order, pure and simple, filled with sensual assurance.

She dragged in a breath, desperate to agree, every inch of her clamouring for the pleasure behind the promise. But she hesitated. They paused outside Clara's ward. He leaned against the wall, his head cocked in challenge, awaiting her answer. They stood a perfectly professional distance apart, but the air between them was thick with pheromones. She might as well be naked and wrapped around him, so intense was his invisible force field drawing her in.

Clara glanced down the corridor, horribly torn. Her body was fully on board but her head couldn't shake off the words of caution. Maybe it was the ticking clock. Maybe it was Sister's reminder of his importance, of how he was regarded public property, how he would soon be promoted to the 'top job'. Maybe it was that pesky reality of hers.

'What if someone sees me at the palace when I'm off-duty?' No one could know.

'We'll meet somewhere after dark,' he said, his eyes sparkling with excitement, making a pulse thrum between her legs. 'We'll leave your car and I'll smuggle you into the palace in mine. I'll text you an out-of-the-way meeting place.'

Clara swallowed, adrenaline a wild rush in her veins, her stare obsessively glued to his sexy mouth. She wanted him too much, the longing also a reason for hesitation.

Being smuggled into the palace on her night off seemed way riskier than that day at the lodge, when she'd already had a legitimate work-related reason to be at the palace. What if she was caught in his suite? She wasn't one of his society sophisticates; she was a normal woman.

With Prince Henrik's diagnosis public knowledge, media speculation and interest in Andreas had sky-rocketed. If anyone got wind of their…affair… if her family shame of her father's notoriety, debts and prison sentence came out, not only would she have to relive the humiliation but Andreas would be tainted by association.

She should tell him, before he found out some other way. But not here. Not now.

'It feels…risky.' She should return to the ward and her duties. Except he was looking at her the way he'd done when she'd been naked, when he'd moved inside her, when he'd watched her climax... triumphantly confident.

As if tired of her caution, Andreas glanced along the corridor and then sprang into action, taking her hand and dragging her into a vacant treatment room. The minute the door closed, she was in his arms, their lips crashing together, their tongues thrusting, their hands restlessly fisting each other's clothes.

His powerful body pinned her to the back of the door, the heat of him a stifling inferno. She rubbed her body against his, seeking the friction that would help quench the fire, but her uniform was too tight; she couldn't open her legs wide enough to have him where she wanted. She clung to him, kissing him back with so much pent-up desire, she would surely leave scorch marks on his white coat.

He growled, pulling back while his greedy hands caressed her hips, her waist, her breasts. 'Please, *sötnos*. I can't spend another night without you. I'm going out of my mind. *You* are the real reason I came in today.'

Before she could answer, he kissed her fiercely once more, his lips then sliding down her neck, hitting all her sensitive spots, coiling the desire between her legs tighter. Clara tried to cling to the elusive threads of her argument, but her brain was paralysed with pleasure. It was as if that day at the cabin had primed her body to respond to him, only him, on reflex. She was panting, slick heat in her pelvis, her drugged-up mind ready to agree to any liaison he suggested.

'I can't think straight for wanting you.' He stroked her nipple through her clothes and she dropped her head back against the door, exposing her neck to his open-mouthed kisses.

This was crazy. They were at work; this room was regularly used. But she couldn't seem to stop kissing him, the thrill of his need for her, of finding him hard, making her bold and, oh, so reckless.

She cupped his erection through his scrubs. He groaned against her skin, the scrape of his facial hair sending shivers through her every nerve. But she couldn't go back to work with stubble rash from his beard. Somehow that thought gave her the strength to shove him back a pace.

'Okay. I'll meet you later,' she said. 'But the location has to be absolutely safe. If I think there's a chance we'll be seen together, I won't stop.'

He braced his hand on the door over her head, and stared down at her with hooded eyes. 'Bring your toothbrush; you'll be staying the night. I need to get my fill of you in case we are forced to spend another week like the last.'

At the thought of spending the entire night in his bed, trickles of elation zapped along her nerves, setting off a series of shudders. 'I can't wait. But now I have to go.'

Yanking his neck, she pressed one last kiss to his lips, which were curled in a self-satisfied smile. She ducked away and checked her reflection in the mirror over the sink. Debauched: there was no other way to describe the flush to her skin, the excitement in her eyes and the kiss-swollen state of her lips.

'Don't you have somewhere to be?' she asked, flicking him an accusing stare in the mirror before splashing her face with cold water.

He leaned against the door they'd just utilised, his arms crossed over his chest while he watched her smugly.

'The interview is in an hour,' he said, looking as if he might reach for her again. 'A public relations exercise dreamt up by the palace—let's show the nation a candid glimpse of the heir doing his day job while he still has it...'

At the defeat in his muttered words, Clara turned to face him. 'I'm sorry.'

'It's fine.' He shrugged, his stare vulnerable, bewildered by the sacrifices he had to make. 'But our secret rendezvous will be the only thing getting me through this afternoon.'

Clara nodded, uncertain what to say. Andreas didn't have to trust her with his feelings on giving up medicine. He'd made it clear at the cabin that her advice that he should talk to Prince Henrik was unwelcome.

'I'll let you get back to work,' he said, carelessly swiping his fingers through his hair. 'Until tonight.'

He opened the door, turning to wink at Clara before he ducked outside.

Clara rushed back to the ward, her stomach knotted with excitement for tonight which, with everything that was going on for him, could be their last.

Either way, he deserved to know her most shameful secret. He deserved to know the risks they were taking with their affair.

She would tell him tonight.

CHAPTER TWELVE

ANDREAS PULLED THE CAR into the underground garage at the palace, his excited pulse a deafening rage in his ears. He was only flesh and blood, and having Clara close enough to touch but still out of reach while he drove had tested his limits to the max.

'Are you sure no one saw me?' she asked from the passenger seat, still ducked down, out of sight.

'Positive,' he said, turning off the engine. 'The windows are tinted.'

He didn't add that he'd asked Nils to do a dry run of their route to ensure there'd be no hidden surprises. Clara was skittish enough without knowing that, since the press release confirming his father's diagnosis, media interest in Andreas had tripled. There was nothing like bad news to fuel speculation about Varborg's future ruler. He'd resolutely avoided watching the news, but he'd been told that several international newspapers were running stories on the tragedy-struck Cronstedt family, rehashing the death of Andreas's mother and Oscar as entertainment for the masses.

He understood Clara's caution. The idea of her facing the kind of public and media interest he'd experienced these past few days, left him chilled to the bone. He'd do everything in his power to safeguard her privacy. He'd vowed to protect her and he wouldn't let her down.

Andreas unclipped his seatbelt. 'Come here.'

He leaned over the centre console, cupping Clara's face to give her the proper kiss he'd had to hold inside for eight endless days. He pressed kisses to her closed eyelids, the tip of her nose, the angle of her jaw and that sensitive place on her neck.

'I missed you so much,' he mumbled against her soft lips, his heart thudding with urgency.

Why had he ever taken his previous freedom and relative privacy for granted? Soon his life would be unrecognisable—every second of his time scheduled, people constantly surrounding him, public appearances and interviews to be done, like this afternoon's. His grip on his old life was slipping, and Clara was the one thing that made his situation tolerable.

He held her tighter. 'I'm adding a new condition—we can't leave it that long again.'

His time for indulging in flings, his time for working alongside Clara, was running out. Every second with her felt precious.

'We've been busy,' she said, pulling him closer so the gear stick jabbed his ribs. 'And we need to be careful at the hospital. No more steamy gropes in the treatment room, although Sister might not let anyone else near you.'

'Right now, I can't think of anything more important than kissing you.' Andreas groaned; she was too far away, had too many clothes on, was talking too much.

But Clara's words had struck a nerve. Constitutionally, he belonged to Varborg. He was obliged to marry, produce an heir, and secure the next generation of Cronstedt princes and princesses. He'd always known it would take an exceptional woman to walk at his side through the circus that would be his life from here on out. But, since meeting Clara, his desires had solidified. He didn't want a cardboard cut-out for a wife. He wanted something real with someone who understood him beyond the public role he played. Someone to grow at his side. Someone he could respect, love and care for.

But right now he only cared about one woman. He breathed in the scent of her skin and slid his hand along her thigh, which was covered in thick black stockings that disappeared under a tight woollen skirt.

She gripped his tie, pulling his mouth back to hers.

'I like you all dressed up,' she said. 'You look extremely hot in an untouchable kind of way. Is this what you wore for the interview?'

'You can touch all you want, *sötnos*.' Andreas grinned, his hand locating an inch of bare skin at her waist. 'But, yes, I wore this for part of the filming. They also had me dress in scrubs and examine a few people at the hospital—make Varborg's heir relatable to the masses.'

Clara slid her fingers through his hair, pushing it

back from his face, staring up at him thoughtfully. 'You are relatable; you don't have to try.'

'Maybe you should be on my PR team.' Andreas gripped her hand and kissed her knuckles one by one. She saw things in him no one else saw; believed in him without agenda.

'If we don't move right now,' he said, reaching for the door handle at his back, 'You'll be riding me in this seat with the steering wheel at your back.'

Spurred into action by Clara's nervous squawk and the desire pounding through his blood, Andreas exited the vehicle and rushed her towards the lift to the guest suite he was still using.

She kissed him again, driving him wild with delicate darts of her tongue against his. 'You won't be able to smuggle me in like this much longer,' she said as they tumbled out of the lift, tugging at each other's clothes, pausing every few steps to kiss. 'Especially when you move into your own suite.'

She shoved at his suit jacket and he tossed it on the floor. 'I'll build a secret tunnel from your house to mine,' he said, only half-joking, 'So you can come to me any time you want.'

He refused to think of them ending when every other aspect of his life was so uncertain.

He *needed* her. She laughed but a shadow crossed her eyes. There was something hesitant about her tonight, more than her fear of discovery. It was making him jittery.

'Why are we wasting time talking,' he said,

'When that's been all we could do for eight excruciating days?'

He reached for her, losing himself in her kisses, gripping her waist and guiding her into the bedroom. Clara pulled the hem of his shirt free of his trousers and slid her hands up his back, restlessly pressing her body against his. He removed her sweater and popped open her bra, his hands greedily caressing her beautiful breasts as they spilled free.

'Because I've missed you,' she said simply, honestly, perfectly.

That was his Clara...

The possessive direction of his thoughts caught him off-guard. She wasn't his. This was a fling; even if he wanted something more permanent, that wasn't what *she* wanted. He didn't want to hurt her, disappoint her or let her down, and his father's diagnosis had curtailed his freedoms. Just as Oscar had done, he must put duty first. He couldn't drag someone as unique and guileless as Clara into his world of ancient protocol and public service. She cherished her independence and her career. He wouldn't change a single thing about her.

Right here, right now, this was all they had because he couldn't fail another person he cared about.

Unease compounded his desperation for her. He quickly peeled the remaining clothes from her body, taking one indulgent second to rake his gaze over her nakedness, his hands skimming her skin as if committing the softness, every dip and swell to memory.

'You're so beautiful; you steal my breath.' He tugged her close, the heat of her burning through his clothes. 'Later, I'm taking you in my giant bath, the scene of our first meeting. But first... I need you.'

He thumbed her nipples erect, smiling when she moaned his name and dropped her head back so he could ravage her neck with kisses.

'I need you too,' she said on a sigh, taking hold of his tie once more and tugging him by the neck towards the bed. She sat down and hurriedly undid his belt and fly, looking up at him with wicked intent. He'd barely survived the last time she put her gorgeous mouth on him. And he was strung so taut, the tick-tock of the clock flooding his body with a sense of panic, that this time he might actually fracture apart.

With a look of thrilling determination, Clara encircled his erection, licked up the length of him and then took him inside her mouth. She hummed a satisfied sound of delight. He closed his eyes, a surge of arousal filling him to bursting point. How could she do this to him—render him unstable with her touch and that look that said she saw him exactly as he was? Just a man.

But there was something wild about her tonight. Had she reached her limit in the eight days they'd been forced apart by work schedules and life? Or was she too hungrily preparing for future famine when they'd be once more forced apart, maybe for good. No; he couldn't think about that.

Spurred into action, he yanked back his hips. He

tossed off his clothes and prosthesis and prowled over her naked body. He kissed her lips, her breasts, her stomach and then dived between her legs to kiss and lick her into a sobbing frenzy. He was addicted to her taste. Addicted to everything, from the stud in her nose to the sharp wit of her tongue and the sound of her moans when she climaxed.

She cried out his name now, her hands twisting in his hair. He teased her sensitive nipples to hard peaks so she was writhing, needy for him, her hands restless and grabby.

'We won't be sleeping tonight,' he said, settling his weight over her. 'I want to make up for those eight days with as many orgasms as is humanly possible.'

He slid his hand to the slick heat between her legs, watching her eyes darken with need.

'Yes…' She dug her nails into his shoulders and spread her thighs wide so their hips aligned.

On fire from within, his heartbeat banged, dangerously high.

'I can't get enough of you,' he panted, tearing his mouth away from her kisses. He cupped her thigh, his hips grinding between her parted legs as if out of his control. He'd never been this hot for a woman. The deprivation had sharpened the ache for her, only her, and one look at her passion-dazed expression told him she felt the same way.

Clara held his face and brought their lips back together in a rush of frantic and deep kisses. She cupped his buttocks, urging him closer, tilting her hips to meet him and shrouding him in her scalding heat as he pushed inside her with a groan of profound relief.

'Andreas!' she cried.

He reared up on his elbows and captured one nipple with his mouth. She crossed her ankles in the small of his back so he sank deeper inside her. Their bodies moved together in a frenzied rhythm as they tried to quench the need riding them both so hard.

How would he ever find the strength to let her go, having taken his entire adult life to find someone so remarkable? In that moment, he could have sworn that Clara was as essential as the very air he breathed.

He rolled them, holding her hips so they stayed locked together. She sat astride him and rode him, her hair a wild tumble around her flushed face. He cupped her pert breasts and stroked her nipples with his thumbs. She shattered, her stare locked to his, her cries ringing out around the room, until he jack-knifed into a sitting position and kissed them up.

With one final roar, he crushed her to his chest and spilled himself inside her, a part of his soul surely branded hers for all eternity.

Clara relaxed back against Andreas's hard chest, so languid in the warm scented bubble bath that she might have fallen asleep if she hadn't been so attuned to every subtle shift of Andreas's touch. They'd lit what seemed like a hundred candles around the bath and left the blinds open so they could look out at the view of the snow-capped mountains and inky night sky.

Her skin tingled with awareness, the throbbing pulse between her legs barely satiated, even after that incredible orgasm. How would she survive the loss of such pleasure when this fling came to an end? And end it must. Clara was an ordinary woman, too cynical for relationships. Even if she'd wanted more from Andreas, it would be an impossible fairy tale. He would rule Varborg, marry his princess and produce his own heirs, and Clara would watch from the side-lines. Although, she had no clue how she would see pictures of him in the media and not want him with this all-encompassing need...

'I'm sorry about the condom, *sötnos*,' he said, pressing his lips to the side of her neck so she shivered with delight.

'I'm sorry too. But, despite having only one previous partner, I'm still on birth control.'

They'd been so wild for each other after their eight days apart, they'd forgotten all about protection.

'I'm normally very sexually responsible,' he said, his hands sliding up and down her thighs under the water. 'You just make me...insatiable.'

'Insatiable, huh?' Clara smiled like the cat that had stolen the cream, the flutters in her chest telling her just how much she trusted Andreas.

Now that they were finally alone, she should tell him about her father's prison sentence. But she was so relaxed, his touch so hypnotic, it was hard to think about anything but him. And, once her secret was out, she'd have nowhere left to hide. That most vulnerable part of herself, the part she'd always protected from hurt by avoiding relationships, would be exposed. He'd know *everything*.

His lips skimmed the sensitive place on her neck, distracting her once more. 'Will you watch my interview when it airs? Let me know how badly it comes across?'

'Of course, but I doubt it will be bad. You're a prince and a doctor, and you're single. Half of Varborg will be in love with you before the show ends.'

Now it was his turn to chuckle, while spikes of jealousy pricked Clara's skin. But he didn't belong to her.

'Did they ask you any questions you didn't want to answer?' she asked to detract from the helpless, jittery feeling in the pit of her stomach.

'I'd already vetoed any questions relating to Oscar's death,' he said. 'But they asked if I'm currently seeking a princess to marry—only to be expected in my position. My personal life is considered public property.'

Clara flinched. Wasn't she temporarily part of his personal life? Because she'd rather have run naked out into the snow than know if Andreas was officially courting some foreign princess or lucky aristocrat closer to home, she latched onto another topic.

'Will you tell me about Oscar?' she whispered,

resting her head on his shoulder so his next kiss landed on her cheek. 'I'd love to know what he was like.'

Andreas took a deep breath, his chest expanding at her back.

'It's so hard to paint one picture,' he said on a sigh. 'He was so many things.'

'Like you, then,' Clara said, lifting his hand to press a kiss to his fingers.

'He was good at everything.' His voice lightened with admiration. 'But somehow humble too. He could ski like a champion, speak five languages and he always had a joke up his sleeve, ready to drop it into conversation if and when appropriate.'

Clara smiled, pressing a breathy kiss to his lips. 'Very useful skills for a statesman. How many languages do *you* speak?'

'Only three, I'm afraid.'

'What a dreadful under-achiever,' she teased, and he laughed. 'Hot and intelligent and kind—the palace may need to ramp up security once that interview airs.' But her teasing cost her another jealous roll of her stomach.

He chuckled. After a few seconds, he stiffened. 'Oscar's death was a great loss for the future of Varborg. He had big plans to modernise the principality. We discussed it often—how things would be different for our children.'

'What kind of plans?' Clara didn't want to imagine Andreas's fair-haired children.

He shrugged, sending out ripples of bathwater.

'Ways to challenge the old guard traditionalists, a more equal distribution of duties between royal siblings, that kind of thing.'

'Things you can still implement yourself, if you choose.' She entwined her fingers with his, cautious of making him withdraw, the way he had at the cabin when she'd pushed too hard.

'I guess. We didn't discuss it until we were adults, but we were both lonely growing up so…segregated. We needed to develop our own interests and be independent, but when it came to our royal life we could have acted as a team rather than being divided. Not that it matters now.'

Clara stilled, aware of the thud of his heart at her back and the matching rhythm in her chest. Every second of their time was precious, but Andreas's past issues with his place in the Cronstedt family were holding him back from being his wonderfully authentic self. He'd made it clear that he wouldn't be addressing those issues with his father. But, if she could get him talking, maybe it would help him to believe in his ability to rule.

'Will you tell me about the accident?' she whispered. 'I promise I'll never speak of it to another soul.'

'I know you won't, *sötnos*.' Andreas pressed his lips to her temple. 'You and I share a sense of loyalty. I trust you.'

Clara swallowed, her eyes stinging with longing. He trusted her but she was hiding something from him: her most shameful family secret. She needed to tell him, and soon.

'Oscar and I were both in the army, in different regiments,' he said, staring ahead as if staring into the past. 'We were attending the same training exercise. It was all perfectly standard until it wasn't. Oscar was in a vehicle crossing rough terrain when it hit a concealed ditch and rolled.'

Clara sat frozen, a shiver running through her, although the water was still warm.

'I heard it on the radio,' he continued. 'The medical corps were training nearby, so we rushed to help. We managed to free the driver, but Oscar was unconscious in the passenger seat, the crushed cab of the vehicle trapping him.'

His heart thudded against her back and Clara gripped his hand tighter, wishing she could undo his pain and loss.

'We cleared the shattered windscreen,' he continued, 'And I half-climbed in so I could preserve Oscar's airway while we waited for the cutting crew. I could tell it looked bad for him. He had an obvious head injury, and a scalp wound that was bleeding profusely, but all I could do in that position was stabilise his neck, pressure-dress the wound and protect his airway.'

Tears tracked down Clara's cheeks. He must have felt so scared and helpless.

'I was too emotionally attached to be objective,' Andreas said. 'But I refused to leave him, even when he went into cardiac arrest. I performed CPR, even when I was ordered to step down by my superior officer so someone else could take over. Even when someone noticed the petrol leaking, I refused to leave my brother.'

Clara turned to face him, the full horror of what must have happened hitting her like a blow.

He nodded, his face pale with grief, as if he was reliving the accident. 'The wreck burst into flames. I was thrown clear, but I broke both my legs.'

'I'm so sorry,' she whispered, pressing her lips to his in silent apology. Why had she asked him? Because she just selfishly wanted to know everything about him, for her own insatiable needs.

'They saved the right leg, but the left was fractured and badly burned, and became infected. They had to amputate three days before Oscar's funeral.'

'Andreas…' She sat astride his lap, holding onto both his hands as if she'd never let go. 'You could have died too.'

He shook his head, dismissing her concern. 'He was my brother, my senior in rank, my country's heir to the throne and I couldn't save him.'

Clara's vision blurred with sadness. She gripped his face. '*No one* could have saved him. You did everything humanly possible. It was a terrible accident.'

'A part of me knows that.' A sad smile tugged his lips; he didn't believe her. 'But the rest of me just feels guilty. I'm a *doctor*. I let him down. And why was it me to survive and not him?'

'You know why.' Clara rested her forehead against his. 'Life is random and sometimes unfair.'

She didn't need to tell Andreas that. He was an intelligent man of the world, a leader, who'd had more than his fair share of family tragedy.

'*He* should be here now,' Andreas said as if he hadn't heard, as he gripped her upper arms so they were locked together in this horrible moment of grief and heartache. 'He was meant to be the one to succeed Prince Henrik.'

Clara shook her head violently. The idea of never having met Andreas was too horrible to contemplate.

'You feel responsible because of your profession,' she said passionately. 'Because he was your big brother, a man you loved and respected; because the family you were born into has a hereditary hierarchy most families don't have. But it wasn't your fault.'

He stared up at her, pain shifting across his beautiful eyes. And something else—need. His arms came around her waist and he held her so close, burying his face against the erratic thud of her heart. It was as if their connection, this wild storm of desire that never seemed to lessen, went way beyond physical in that moment.

But it couldn't. She wouldn't let it mean more. She was strong. She would be there for him, embrace their intimacies until it was time for them to part and then she'd deal with the fallout once it was over.

Clara stroked his hair and held him to her heart as if she could fix the broken pieces of him. His life was in turmoil. He was grieving for the past and the future. He was hurting, carrying unnecessary guilt over Oscar's death and feeling that he was second best to a dead man because of his family's succession, and because he had unresolved issues with Prince Henrik. If what he'd told her the day at the cabin was true, he and Prince Henrik had never really spoken about Oscar's death. Perhaps if Andreas knew that no one else blamed him, including his father, he could start to forgive himself. It might ease his struggles with the royal role he felt he didn't deserve.

But, just like Andreas hadn't been able to save Oscar, Clara couldn't save Andreas. He needed to do that himself.

'What can I do to help you?' she asked, aching for him.

His arms tightened around her waist. 'You help me simply by being here. Things make sense when I'm with you. You understand me. You see me, the real me. You always have.'

Clara held him while he crushed her to him.

Right now, while the rest of his life was tugging him in all directions, he might feel as if he needed her, but she couldn't forget her reality. Her valued independence, her own shameful past and her determination for equality in any future relationship.

'I know you think I should talk to the prince about the past, about Oscar,' he continued. 'And maybe you're right. But, what with my crash course on ruling Varborg, stepping in to fulfil most of my father's engagements and planning a state funeral in minute detail, the prince and I already have many things on our minds.'

'I'm sorry. I didn't mean to pry.' Her voice sounded sickeningly small, the feeling she'd been dismissed once more causing a hot ache in her throat. It made memories of her final phone call to her father resurface, when he'd trivialised her concerns and refused to make her any promises.

But she didn't need promises from Andreas. This was just sex.

'And I didn't mean to offload.' He dragged her lips to his. 'Let's forgive each other.'

Clara nodded and smiled, because he'd done nothing wrong. He was just dealing with his lot in life in the best way he knew how. It wasn't Andreas's fault that she'd learned from her own regrets or that she would hate to see him miss his chance to heal some of the scars holding him back before his father died. But she needed to accept that sometimes she just couldn't fix what was broken.

'I've handed in my notice at Nordic Care,' he said, looking up at her with such grief and vulnerability, she shoved aside her selfish thoughts on what that would mean for her.

'That's good.' She pressed her lips to his. 'You have a lot going on.'

But she understood his reluctance to end his locum job. He was clinging to the one thing he could control, the one thing he could ensure he was good at—his career.

But he had so much more to give.

'You're like your brother, Andreas,' she said imploringly. 'You'll be good at anything you set your mind to, including ruling this nation of ours.'

His expression shifted from despair to bewilderment. 'You asked how you could help...and my answer is just be yourself. Don't ever change, *sötnos*.'

He brushed her lips with his on a ragged sigh, pulling back to search her stare. 'You are the only good thing I can hold onto right now.' His hands restlessly skimmed her back and her shoulders, his fingers tunnelling into her hair. 'I need you, Clara. I want you.'

Gripping the back of her neck, he dragged her mouth back to his. His kiss grew deeper, his hands roaming her body as if he was committing the shape of her to memory.

Clara surrendered, kissing him back, losing herself again. Every time she veered away from the passion and connection they found in each other's arms, she came unstuck, her mind spinning out, searching for answers and solutions that were right there in front of her.

For, however long they had left, *this* was all that mattered.

His hands gripped her hips under the water, drawing her close. He was hard between her legs. Rising up on her knees, she guided him inside her body, each of them sighing with relief as they stared into each other's eyes.

For now, he was hers—her wild mountain-man, her Viking.

As she rocked above him and he moved inside her, passion spiralling as they clung to each other, and Clara clinging to the only part of him she could have, she promised herself she would hold something back.

She would protect her heart the way she'd always done because, of all men, Andreas had the power to do the most damage.

CHAPTER THIRTEEN

THREE DAYS LATER, Clara was just about to leave the palace after her night shift when she received a text from her sister, Freja.

Have you seen this?

The message accompanied a link to a celebrity news site. The main article featured a grainy picture of Andreas and Clara kissing goodbye at her car the morning after she'd spent the night in his bed at the palace.

Her stomach dropped at the sickening headline: *How Much Longer Can the Heir Play the Field?*

Horrified, her pulse went through the roof. She could almost taste the public's rejection, hear their judgement and contempt that she wasn't good enough for Varborg's heir. But, worse, if her identity was revealed, if the connection between Lars Lund and her got out, her family's humiliating past might hurt Andreas at a time when he must feel as if his life was falling apart.

Tears pricked her eyes. Her father's disgrace shouldn't be her burden to bear, but she'd been hardwired most of her life to feel the sting of rejection. And that guilty part of her, that should have already come clean to Andreas, now had nowhere left to hide.

It was time to face him.

Willing herself to calm down, Clara texted Andreas.

We need to talk.

Against her better judgement, she scoured the picture again. The photographer had clearly been hiding some distance away, using a telephoto lens. Clara was only visible from behind, but her parked car was in the background. The registration number had been blurred out, but it would only take some nosy journalist a few seconds of sleuthing to find out her identity and the paper trail of shame that would lead to her door.

Andreas's reply was swift.

Come to the green sitting room in the family wing. Sorry, I can't get away.

With acid burning her throat, Clara hurried to the room she knew of but had never been inside, grateful for the sense of legitimacy her uniform provided.

Her rapid steps matched the panicked bounding of her heart. What if poor Prince Henrik had seen the photo? What if the palace press office was aware of the identity of Andreas's unsuitable mystery woman? Would she be fired or banned from seeing Andreas?

An ache settled under her ribs, its potency suspicious of grief. But she'd always known this day would come, that she'd have to give him up; she'd just hoped for a little more time. Knocking on the door, she waited for the call to enter and then ducked quickly inside.

He wasn't alone.

Even with a firestorm of fear in her veins, her heart lurched at the arresting sight of Andreas. His immaculately tailored navy suit caressed his lean and sculpted body to perfection. He looked up from adjusting his crisp white cuffs, which glinted with onyx cuff links, his stare burning into hers from across the room.

Taking one look at Clara's face, Andreas stiffened.

'Leave us,' he instructed the valet, who ceased his efforts brushing invisible specks of lint from Andreas's suit and hastily fled.

'What is it, *sötnos*?' A small frown tugged down his mouth as he crossed the room.

Clara rested her eyes on his, her heart actually stuttering to a stop. The flood of desire for him was almost strong enough to dispel her profound embarrassment—almost.

Last night, snuggled on the sofa with her mum and Freja, with mugs of hot chocolate, she'd watched Andreas's interview. She'd sat spellbound, her eyes glued to the screen as the skilled programmers painted a portrait of Andreas the doctor, Andreas the veteran, Andreas the heir.

Now, chilled to the bone, she was fooling herself

to think she could have any part of such a magnificent man. He was wildly dashing, every inch the eligible prince and commanding statesman he feared he might never be. But he couldn't fight his upbringing, his genetics and the historic breeding of his family line. He was a prince. He always had been, from the day he'd been born. Clara had just forgotten that, allowing herself to be swept along by lust, by her professional regard and the way he'd made her feel special. But *he* was the special one.

'You're scaring me, Clara.' He gripped her upper arms. 'Are you hurt? Is it Prince Henrik?'

Clara shook her head and blurted out her reason for disturbing him. 'There's a photo of us together online.'

She blinked to stave off tears; her revelation would be final confirmation that this was over. Had she already tarnished his reputation by association? And at a time when he had so much else going on.

A muscle clenched in his jaw, but he didn't seem surprised. 'I've been made aware.' He reached for her hands. 'I'm sorry. The announcement of Prince Henrik's state of health has, I'm afraid, caused an increased interest in my personal life.'

She frowned, her head foggy with desire, confusion and guilt. Could she blame the public? She too had watched the candid thirty-minute interview of Varborg's heir with rapt fascination bordering on obsession, her hot drink forgotten.

'No, *I'm* sorry.' She tugged her hands from his,

feeling shabby and creased in her uniform, more aware than ever before of their massive differences.

With his face cloaked in his signature close-cropped beard, he was more handsome rogue than prince of the realm, but of course that was a massive part of his Viking appeal.

He frowned. 'Why are *you* apologising? It's me they were after, not you.' He ran a hand through his tamed hair. '*I* should be the one apologising for not protecting you better, for exposing you to the seedier side of life in the public gaze. I know you wanted to keep us a secret. For now, they don't seem to know who you are.'

His hands gripped her elbows and he pressed a desperate kiss to her lips. Clara's body reacted, as always, to his kiss.

'You don't understand,' she said, extricating herself from his touch. She wanted nothing more than to curl up in his arms and hide from her past, from the ugliness and risk she'd exposed him to. But shame was a painful gripe in her belly.

'I understand all too well.' His voice rose, fury sparking in his grey stare. 'It's an invasion of my privacy and yours. *I* expect it, but they have no right to target you. I won't let that happen. I swear to you, Clara. I'll protect you.'

'I need to tell you something.' Clara shook her head, trying to stay on track, but shock and desire threatened to derail her thoughts. She could no longer deny that her need for this man was now a full-blown addiction. She'd realised that last night, watching him on the screen.

'*Sötnos...*' He stepped closer and wrapped her in his arms so she was engulfed by his warmth and the scent of his cologne. 'Please don't distress yourself over this. Let me deal with it. I have people. I'll ensure that you remain anonymous.'

He tilted her chin, brushing his thumb over her bottom lip, his stare dipping there. 'It's just a fishing expedition—social commentary from strangers who don't know me but think I should be married by now, or some such rubbish.'

Clara recoiled from his touch, turning her head away. The idea of Andreas with another woman hit her like a slap to the face. But of course there would be other women after her, until finally his princess: a sophisticated beauty with the appropriate pedigree, well-schooled in dealing with press intrusion, her closet devoid of tawdry family skeletons. The kind of woman who would look at home on the arm of the immaculate and urbane prince before her.

Hating her own weakness, her self-doubt-fuelled envy, Clara snapped, 'I don't need you to rescue me or protect me; I can take care of myself.'

Andreas frowned, his gaze flicking to the clock on the wall. 'So it's okay for you to want to help me, but not for me to help you?'

Clara dragged in a calming breath. He clearly had places to be, important people to see. Her sad family drama would be swiftly passed to some lackey in the palace press office.

'I won't keep you,' Clara said, rolling back her shoulders, 'But I need you to listen. I told you about my father running out on us, but the bit I left out was that he was something of a swindler. Not only did he get into all kinds of debt while my parents were together, he also re-mortgaged our family home behind my mother's back. But the worst thing he did was defraud a bunch of people in some sort of pyramid scheme. He went to prison, Andreas. He died in prison. That's why I never had the chance to confront him, because I refused to visit.'

'Clara—'

'I know I should have told you before.' She blinked, refusing to cry for the father who'd let her down so badly. 'But I'm not exactly proud of the fact. I thought, if we were careful, it never needed to come out.'

'It doesn't matter,' he stated flatly, moving towards her and then stopping, presumably in response to her expression.

'Of course it matters,' she snapped, her fears spilling free. 'We promised we'd be careful, but now look what's happened. I'm...news. I never wanted any of this. I just wanted *you*.'

'I'm right here.' He gripped her cold hand and rested it over his chest where his heart thudded against her palm, vibrant and steady.

Clara looked away from his impeccable appearance; he felt more out of reach than ever. 'And you may as well be on the moon, don't you see?' she cried. 'We've always been too different and now the whole world will see that. You'll be embarrassed. Prince Henrik will be embarrassed. Neither of you need a scandal right now.'

She tugged her hand free and backed away from him. She couldn't think when he touched her—that was how they'd ended up in this mess.

'I'll probably lose my job,' she continued, 'And my mother has been through enough without having the whole sordid story regurgitated.'

Tension built in the silence as she finally faced him.

'Are you ending this?' A fierce scowl slashed his handsome face. 'Because I know what I need, and I told you, it's you.'

Confused, Clara shook her head. For a brief moment, him, their connection had been the one easy thing she'd wanted. But it was no longer easy.

'I'm not sure we ever really got started,' she said sadly. She didn't want to leave him, not yet. 'But this photograph certainly complicates things.'

'I told you, I'll take care of it,' he said.

'How? You're royalty,' she argued, deaf to his promises. In Clara's experience, believing in those only made you more vulnerable. 'If people find out you're fraternising with the penniless daughter of a convicted criminal, it could damage your reputation!'

'Don't do this.' He gripped her face, staring at her with panic in his eyes. 'Don't let strangers come between us.'

Tilting her mouth up, he delivered a crushing kiss

as if he could make her believe in him, that he'd deal with the issue.

Her lips parted on a shocked gasp. His tongue surged into her mouth, coaxing. Because she'd always been helpless to their desire for each other, Clara's brain shut down, her body clinging to the pleasure of his kiss to block out all the ugliness in which she felt coated.

This beautiful man, who could have any woman, wanted *her*. The power of it surged through her. *This*, them together, made sense and blocked out reality.

His fingers tangled in her hair, spilling it loose from its bun. His body heat scorched her. His hard chest brushed her sensitive nipples, his thigh pressing between her legs as he backed her up against a table. There was an ominous rattle of something heavy, perhaps a lamp, but Clara was too inflamed to care. She clung to him, drowning, so far out of her depth with this man that her only certainty was that she should walk away. But it was as if her heart knew best and wanted him, no matter what.

'Andreas,' she moaned, spearing her fingers through his hair as he trailed kisses down her neck and slid one hand up her thigh, under her uniform and into her underwear. 'You have to go,' she gasped, palming his erection through his trousers, aware that she was holding him up for whatever important princely engagement he was immaculately dressed.

'I don't care.' He shoved down her underwear and

unbuckled his belt. 'I only care about you. About this. About us.'

Frantic now with desire, Clara tackled his fly, freeing him from the confines of his suit.

'You can't leave me, not yet.' With a grunt, he hauled her around the waist and deposited her backside on the edge of the table. He kissed her again, his fingers working her nipple through her uniform and bra.

'I won't,' she cried as they broke free of their kisses to fumble together.

Clara hiked up her skirt and spread her thighs. Andreas shoved down his trousers, just enough to free him from his underwear.

'Soon. I'll let you go soon,' he said, staring into her eyes as he pushed inside her. A low growl rumbled in the back of his throat. His hands clutched at her waist, hips and breasts with thrilling heated possession.

'I want you, Clara...' He groaned against her neck, thrusting inside her. 'You asked me what I needed and the answer is *this. You.*'

He pulled back, stark need in his eyes.

'I want you too.' Clara sighed and shuddered, gripping his hips with her thighs and clinging to him as they rode this storm of need together.

'Tell me you're still mine, *sötnos*,' he muttered between kisses, his hands holding her hips so tightly, she wondered if he'd leave marks. 'Tell me we're still in this together—different but equals. Tell me.'

His thrusts grew more frantic, his kisses deep

and demanding, his eye contact so intense, Clara could only hold on and give him her all in return.

'I'm yours,' Clara said, stifling her cries against his lips as pleasure shook her from head to toe, heightened by the glitter of triumph and possession in his stare.

Andreas gave a rough cry and crushed her in his arms as they climaxed together, the furious need finally abating. For long seconds they stayed locked together, hearts thudding, breaths panting.

He moved first, slipping from her body. He stepped back, helping her slide from the table. He buttoned up and Clara shakily scooped her underwear from the floor, stepping inside the garment while her mind raced and her body tried to recover.

What was she doing? She was out of control for this man: risking her emotions; making him promises she might not have the strength to keep; giving him everything when she'd vowed to hold something back as a shield around her inexperienced heart.

He touched her hand and she looked up. Apart from slightly dishevelled hair and a bit of colour on his cheekbones, he was still perfect, still achingly beautiful, still a prince. Sadness, maybe even pity, touched his eyes. 'I've always known about your father, Clara.'

Horrified, she frowned, searching his stare for the truth as ice shifted through her veins.

Andreas's beautiful mouth flattened into a grim

line. 'No one works for my family without a police check and a background check.'

He'd known…all this time? For all his talk of equality…

'You consented to be vetted when you landed the job,' he explained. 'Palace security investigate everyone who works here: their past, their family and their employment history. It's all thoroughly scrutinised.' His lip curled with the barest hint of distaste. 'The price you pay for any association with me, I'm afraid. I wish it wasn't necessary, just like I wish I could spare you the paparazzi.'

He shrugged with sad inevitability.

Clara shrivelled inside, as if what they'd just done had left her dirty. She looked away from him, their differences neon-bright, and the trust she'd foolishly imagined shattered on the floor like shards of glass.

'Why didn't you say anything?' Humiliation burned her eyes as she forced herself to look at him.

All this time she'd thought that on some level they were equals, just Clara and Andreas enjoying their chemistry, but in reality he'd always held all of the power in the relationship.

'It didn't matter to me,' he said flatly. '*You* did nothing wrong. It's like you said the first time we met—our scars don't define us.'

The lump in her throat expanded. How could she have been so naïve?

Andreas raised her chin. 'If you care for me at all, please don't let them come between us. We know who we are, what we value, and we know each other. You know me, Clara. If I say it doesn't matter to me, it doesn't matter.'

Numb, Clara nodded. She *did* know this man. She knew her feelings for him were reckless. She knew he'd seen the deeply vulnerable part of her that she'd always kept guarded. She knew that, if she wasn't careful with her heart, she could fall for him and he could destroy her.

I'll let you go soon...

She winced, hating the words she'd been too pleasure-drunk to analyse when he'd spoken them earlier. She didn't want to be *this* Clara: uncertain, emotionally exposed, scared. She wanted to be her old self, the woman who could take care of herself, needed no one and had her life all figured out.

'I need to go,' she said, clearing her throat. 'I have to drive home and change and head to Nordic Care. I'm doing a late shift.'

He cupped her face. 'I'll take care of the press. Trust me.'

She nodded numbly, kissing him and then moving to the door. She *did* trust him, but it changed nothing. She'd let Andreas too close. She'd wanted him and he'd wanted her and their fling had seemed harmless. But danger was everywhere, overwhelming.

At the door, she turned to look at him one last time. His back was to her. He checked his watch, tugging on his cuffs, and pressed a buzzer on the desk, presumably summoning the valet once more.

He was unspeakably beautiful. The demands on

him were staggering. She'd wanted to ease his burdens, not add to them. She'd wanted to be there for him, not rely on him. She'd wanted to enjoy their affair and then walk away unscathed.

But it was like he'd once said: 'you don't always get what you want'.

CHAPTER FOURTEEN

ANDREAS'S FINAL SHIFT at Nordic Care arrived two days later, much sooner than planned. With a heavy, grieving heart, he strode onto Clara's ward, his eyes scanning for sight of her. Even now, when tension seemed to colour their every interaction, he selfishly craved her like a drug.

Curtains were drawn around the bed of one of his patients. From the urgent comings and goings, Andreas surmised some sort of emergency was taking place. Curious, he entered the bay. Clara, the ward sister and the new registrar, Dr Nilsen, attended to an elderly man, who was breathless.

'Hello, Mr Hagen.' He addressed the patient he'd admitted a week earlier with uncontrolled diabetes and infected venous ulceration of the lower leg, and looked to Clara for guidance as to the nature of the emergency.

Their eyes met. Pressure built in his chest. He'd missed her so much. Her obvious concern for their patient triggered his protective urges. How he ached to comfort her, to spirit them both away—maybe to the hunting lodge so they could be alone, and work out everything that felt tense between them since she'd panicked about her father, and go to bed until the pieces of his world slotted back into place.

But there was no time for any of that.

'What's the situation?' he asked, scanning the monitors. The patient was clearly in respiratory distress, his respiratory rate elevated and his blood oxygen saturations ninety-four percent.

Clara frowned, as if he had no right to be there. 'Acute shortness of breath. Dr Nilsen was on the ward.' She looked away.

'Good, but I know this patient well.' Stifling an irrational flinch of rejection, Andreas took the man's pulse, which was fast but regular, noting the fine beads of sweat on his brow. That Clara had bypassed him and gone straight to another doctor irked. It shouldn't matter, but it was another sign of her dwindling trust. Not that he could blame her; after today, he wouldn't even work at Nordic Care.

'I think it's acute left ventricular failure,' the registrar said while Clara silently passed Andreas an ECG tracing.

'Any chest pain?' Andreas asked, reaching for his stethoscope to listen to Mr Hagen's lungs.

'No,' Clara answered, while the registrar set about siting an intravenous cannula in the man's antecubital fossa.

Andreas listened to the patient's chest, hearing the unmistakeable crackle of pulmonary oedema, or fluid in the lower lobes of the lungs.

'Let's get some intravenous diuretic and morphine, please, Nurse Lund,' he said, taking control of the situation while trying not to draw parallels with his first day there a few short weeks ago.

So much had happened since they'd met, kissed and faced their first emergency together. He felt as if he'd known Clara a lifetime. But how did *she* feel? Did she still relate to the real him, or was she too overwhelmed by the inconveniences of his public life to keep sight of what they'd shared?

Clara left the bay to fetch the medication, returning with two vials and a syringe, which she handed to the registrar, who quickly drew up the drugs and injected them through the IV cannula.

She couldn't even look at him. It was as if she'd already made up her mind and deemed him too much trouble. Andreas concealed his sigh. He might want to protect her, but he couldn't make any guarantees. He didn't want to let her down or fail her in any way.

'Have you listened to Mr Hagen's chest?' he asked, handing over his stethoscope.

The patient's distress eased as the drugs worked. 'Nurse Lund is going to have a listen, Mr Hagen.'

They'd always collaborated on cases and trusted each other's clinical skills and diligence, regardless of the traditional role demarcations of doctor and nurse. They were a team. He wasn't about to act differently now that his personal circumstances dictated that his other job, the one he would inherit, demanded more of his time.

'We need a chest X-ray, bloods and an echo.' He addressed the team. 'He also needs a catheter to monitor urine output. I'll speak to cardiology, make an urgent referral. We need to exclude a silent myocardial infarction.'

There was a flurry of activity, a dividing up of the tasks. Andreas explained the diagnosis and the tests he's ordered to Mr Hagen, and then sat at a computer station to write in the patient's notes.

He kept one eye on Clara while she went about her duties but she wouldn't meet his eye. He'd just finished speaking to his cardiology colleagues when he spied her heading for the ward exit with her bag slung over her shoulder.

He caught up with her just as she left the ward. 'Clara, can we talk?'

She cast a wary glance around the foyer before pushing through the door to the stairwell, a place of relative privacy.

'Why didn't you call me about Mr Hagen?' he asked when the door closed, unable to keep the hurt or accusation from his voice. He stood as close as he dared, desperate to reach for her. But she was rigid and remote.

'I assumed you were busy,' she said, her expression hurt. 'I understand that today is your last day at Nordic Care.' She shrugged, resigned. 'Hospital rumour mill.'

Andreas winced, reaching for her bare arm, the feel of her skin a jolt of desire to his system. 'I'm sorry. I meant to tell you. I've been stuck in A and E most of the morning. The seasonal flu rush has started.'

'It's fine.' She shook her head, her cheeks flushed, as if she was embarrassed by her hurt feelings.

Despair gripped his throat. He stepped closer, dropping his voice. 'You know how I've struggled with giving up work. I've tried to delay the inevitable as long as possible.'

She nodded. 'I understand. You don't have to explain.'

'Yes, I *do*,' he muttered, willing her to look at him properly.

She was slipping through his fingers.

'Everything came to a head this morning,' he said, desperate to downplay the matter so she didn't get too spooked and end this right now. 'More leaks to the press about Father's radiotherapy, speculation about how long he has left. The palace communication team are scrambling to control the flow of information, but tensions are high.'

Sometimes he felt as if his entire world was crumbling. He swallowed, relieved to see the compassion in her stare. 'It's finally forced me to face facts.' He took her hand, needing to touch her. 'I can no longer spread myself so thinly.'

'Of course you can't.' Clara tilted her head in understanding and concern. 'And the demands on you are only going to increase.'

Andreas clenched his jaw in frustration. He wished they were anywhere but there, where they could barely look at each other for fear of discovery, let alone have a meaningful conversation.

'Can you come over tonight?' he asked with

a desperate edge to his voice that he hoped she wouldn't hear. 'We can talk, in private.'

'I finish at six…' She hesitated, glancing down at her feet. 'But perhaps we should…cool it off for a while.'

'This again…?' With his pulse pounding in panic, he rested his hand on her waist, as if he could physically stop her withdrawing. But lately every time they were together felt as if it might be the last time.

'Look, all this media fuss will die down,' he said, willing her to trust him enough to overlook the gossip. 'I know you're nervous about exposure, but I'm dealing with it. I won't let you down.'

Her trust had been badly damaged in the past, so it was no wonder she struggled to completely trust a man like him: a man with baggage. A man whose life was public property.

But couldn't she see that he'd move mountains to protect her?

She sighed, her eyes on their clasped together hands. 'There have been…whisperings on the ward. I think people recognised me from that photo.' She looked up, her fear and uncertainty etched into her face. 'I still need to work here after you've gone, Andreas.'

Nausea rolled through his gut. She was right—after today, he wouldn't be at work to collaborate with her or to be there for her. He didn't want to leave Nordic Care and leave Clara to the wolves. He wanted to look after her. That was what people did when they cared about someone. That was what

Clara herself did all the time: with her patients, her family, even with Andreas.

Except, just like the rest of his life, her trust in him, the connection they'd shared, seemed to be crumbling before his eyes. Without even trying, he was failing her.

'I'm sorry,' he said simply, because he couldn't make her any promises. He had to leave his career. 'I know it's a lot to take on. Of course you must protect yourself.'

With Prince Henrik's diagnosis, with a change of ruler imminent, the media heat on Andreas was only likely to increase. No matter how much he wanted to protect Clara, he was sickeningly aware that, unless she was part of his life, what he could do to keep her family and her safe and safeguard their privacy was limited.

Maybe that was the solution... But she didn't *want* his help.

Fear laced his blood. He'd dated women in the past who'd ended the relationship because they wanted no part of life in the public eye. He'd hoped Clara was different—that she understood him, saw the role, the stage, the act, for what it was: something he did, not something he was. Desperation for her raced through his blood. He didn't want to lose her over this.

'You know all that stuff,' he said, his voice close to begging, 'The media, the photos, the PR moves— that's not the real me. It's just a role I put on, the same way we put on our roles as doctor and nurse when we put on our white coat and uniform.'

'I know.' She inclined her head, regarding him with sad eyes. 'And I've always understood that you have other priorities beyond me.' Her hand rested on his arm. 'I walked willingly into this affair. This isn't a bid for my share of your attention.'

'And just because I'm leaving here sooner than I planned,' he argued, 'Doesn't mean that I'm walking away from *us*. We can still see each other.'

His teeth ground together with frustration. He was already failing at his career and his royal role. And, by selfishly craving Clara, he'd exposed her to speculation, letting her down too.

His stomach dropped. Maybe he should do the right thing and let her go...

He would hate to drag her name into the press and then have her snubbed or criticised for not fitting some arbitrary mould. In his eyes, she was perfect just as she was.

'I'm just trying to be realistic,' she said. 'We agreed it was temporary.'

'Damn realistic,' he snapped, dragging her into his arms and kissing her, his misery finally spilling over. 'Give me a little longer, *sötnos*.'

He was full-blown begging now, his heart pounding against hers as she looked up at him with uncertainty.

A door below them opened, footsteps echoing on the stairs.

Clara stepped out of his embrace, a guilty look on her face. 'I'll try.'

Casting him one last inscrutable look, she descended the stairs and disappeared. Andreas curled his fingers into fists. He'd always known it would take a special woman to tolerate his life. Since they'd begun their affair, he'd experienced brief flashes of inspiration when he'd wondered if Clara might be that very woman.

But now... Was he failing her? Did he risk hurting her by asking her to stay? A man in his position, with the eyes of the world watching and the weight of a nation on his shoulders—not to mention the self-imposed burden of honouring both his father and his brother as the future of Varborg's monarchy—couldn't afford to be wrong about anything, including Clara.

He couldn't bear to make a mistake. If he wasn't careful, he'd let Clara down. He'd let himself down. And he'd let Oscar down.

None of that was an option.

CHAPTER FIFTEEN

LATER THAT EVENING, shaken from the power of her orgasm, Clara clung to Andreas, certain that she'd never let him go. His groan died against her neck where he'd pressed so many passionate kisses she felt sure he'd leave a mark on her skin.

Not that she cared. The reckless part that was wild for him welcomed a sign of his possession. A reminder that, for a brief time, this connection she'd never felt with anyone else had been real.

He pulled back, slipping from her body, looking down to where she was sprawled on the sofa. This time, they hadn't even made it to the bedroom. Even when they were about to discuss the end of their fling, they couldn't keep their hands off each other.

But Clara was a realist. Their time together was coming to an end. Despite the ache in her heart, and the confusion slashed across Andreas's beautiful face, she smiled up at him sadly.

'It's not over, Clara,' he said defiantly, his breaths gusting. 'Not by a long shot.'

He tucked himself back into his jeans and zipped up.

Close to tears, her blood still thick with endorphins, Clara scooped up her underwear from the floor and wordlessly replaced the garment. She needed to be fully clothed for this talk.

'Maybe not.' She stood and moved away, desperate to escape him and the scent of sex, the cloud of pheromones urging her to keep her mouth shut and get lost in his arms once more. 'But we knew it wasn't going to last for ever. We *agreed.*'

'I understand you're scared for your family's reputation,' he said, his tone that of a coaxing parent for a frightened child, 'But I could protect you, all of you.'

'How?' she asked, incredulous. 'Because, of course I'm scared. My family have been through enough and so have yours. I work here. I still have to face Prince Henrik, and I don't want Mum to have to relive the shame of my father's conviction. But it feels as if it's only a matter of time before it's all dredged up in public.'

'There are vacant properties on the estate.' He reached for her, gripping her upper arms. 'You could all move in until interest in my personal life dies down. The press couldn't get to you there.'

Clara frowned, horrified, her heart cracking that he understood her so little. 'Listen to what you're suggesting. Us moving into a palace property would be confirmation that you and I are involved in some sort of seedy tryst. And my mother and I would still need to leave to go to work and my sister to college.'

'Clara…' He cupped her face and stared into her eyes. 'I have more money than I'll ever know what to do with. I can support you and your family, indefinitely.'

Clara yanked herself free. 'Are you suggesting that I give up my job too? And what—be a kept woman, waiting in some hidden away cottage for your clandestine visits when you have a break in your important schedule or when the royal itch requires scratching?'

'Stop.' His voice was low but authoritative, his scowl the only sign of his fury. 'It wouldn't be like that. I'm not suggesting for ever. I'm just trying to help, because I care about you.'

'I care about you too.' Clara paced out of his reach, suddenly too hot *and* too cold. 'But I told you from the start—I need my independence.'

She levelled him with a defiant stare. 'I watched Mum take second place to my father, quietly toiling away to put food on the table while he chased dream after dream, scheme after scheme, only to put us more and more in debt. I never understood how she could forgive him, time and again. How nothing he did seemed to destroy her love.'

'I'm not your father.' He scrubbed a hand through his already dishevelled hair. 'I'm not trying to steal your independence. I just don't want this to end over one grainy photo online. I thought you understood me, my life, my dreams, the part of me the public don't get to see. I showed you all of me.'

'I *do* understand you.' She rushed back to him because she just couldn't stay away. 'I don't want this to end either.' Hot tears pricked the back of her eyes. The situation was impossible and always had been—a hopeless fantasy.

But, for Clara, it wasn't just fear of exposure. There were other more terrifying feelings making her irrational and confused. She'd opened up to Andreas and become vulnerable in a way she'd never been with another person. She'd told him her most shameful family secrets. She'd worked with him, laid in his arms and held him through his struggles and grief.

Despite all her tough self-talk and caution, all her warnings about holding something back, she'd somehow fallen in love with him. And she was scared, so scared.

As if he knew the tender contents of her heart, he reached for her, roughly tugging her into his arms, pressing his mouth to hers with fierce and desperate possession. Clara embraced the kiss, her tongue surging to meet his, squeezing her eyes tightly shut as if she could block out the rest of the world and just be with him like this: just the two of them, no intrusions, no expectations, no fear.

When they were intimate, everything seemed to make sense. But the minute it was over she couldn't help but see how strongly she was kidding herself. She wasn't the woman for him, not long term. Having him would mean losing her independence. She wouldn't become like her mother, loving a man on whom she couldn't depend. Abandoning the hard-working provider Clara had become out of necessity would not only make her reliant, it would shatter any hope of Andreas and her being equals. She might love him, but if she let go of that hope she would struggle to love and respect herself.

And the longer she stayed, the greater the risk that she'd break when this ended. Wasn't it better to go now, on *her* terms?

They broke apart, panting.

Clara shook her head. 'I can't do it,' she whispered. 'I can't be this needy, frightened version of myself. I can't rely on you, or anyone, don't you see that?' Not when he could never love her in return. It would be too great a sacrifice.

Pain shifted through his eyes. 'Can't or won't? All I'm hearing are excuses. You can still be yourself and want me as I am. I'm not trying to change you, or contain you, or clip your wings. You said you wanted us to be equals, but maybe it's *me* you find wanting.'

Clara shook her head, hot licks of shame flooding her face. He was right: they were similar, both broken, damaged and scarred. Her fear was compounding his because he was scared to embrace the role he'd been born for: scared to fail his nation, his dying father and maybe even his beloved Oscar.

Just then, the room's intercom connected.

'Your Highness, there's been an accident in the Banquet Hall. Someone fell from a ladder while decorating for the Christmas party. Can you come?'

Without hesitation, Andreas marched to the intercom, pressed the connection button and spoke. 'I'll be there. Call an ambulance.'

He rushed to the bedroom and returned seconds later with his medical bag.

'I'll come with you,' Clara said. No matter what their personal issues, they were still a team.

He paused at the door, as if about to point out that her presence at the palace when she was off duty would expose their secret affair, but he said nothing.

Clara shoved aside her fears. She loved him and she couldn't have him. What was a little workplace humiliation compared to that?

The Banquet Hall had been transformed by two enormous Christmas trees, and twinkling festive garlands hung from every column and doorway. The casualty, a woman in her fifties, was surrounded by a small group of concerned staff members.

Clara and Andreas kneeled at her side.

'She's unconscious,' Clara said, feeling for breath.

'There's a pulse,' Andreas replied.

'She's barely breathing,' Clara added, seeing an obvious compound fracture of her lower leg.

Andreas produced a bag and mask from his medical case, which he placed over the woman's mouth and nose, and began rhythmically inflating her lungs with air.

'Can you stabilise her neck?' He glanced at Clara. 'She might have a spinal fracture.'

Clara held the woman's head steady while Andreas continued to inflate her lungs. Their eyes met, their concerns shared. Any movement could destabilise a fractured vertebra. But, until the paramedics arrived with a neck splint, all they had was each other.

'Has an ambulance been called?' Andreas asked the nearby staff in a choked voice.

Several of them nodded.

'Can someone get a clean towel from housekeeping?' he instructed, his face pale and slashed with worry. 'And cover that leg wound, please.'

Clara's throat tightened. Andreas seemed frantic.

'Do you know her name?' Clara whispered, her bruised and battered heart going out to him.

'Kari. She's worked here over twenty years. She's always in charge of the staff Christmas party. I... I've met her grandchildren.'

He clearly felt responsible for this woman.

Clara stared at his anguished face, trying to communicate her support without words. Personally, things between them were horribly uncertain, the emotional divide widening with their mismatched expectations and the things holding them back, but she was still there for him.

'Can we have some privacy, please?' Andreas spoke with authority to the onlookers. 'Jens and Magda, you stay. The rest of you, thank you for your help, but we'll take it from here.'

When they were alone, the two remaining staff members having moved a short distance away, Andreas swallowed, his expression pained. 'Thank you for being here. I appreciate your support.'

'It was an accident,' Clara whispered, knowing that he would torture himself if something serious happened to this member of his staff, a woman he'd known most of his life. She knew him so well, this Viking of hers. And the last thing Clara wanted was to add to his burdens. Maybe she could hold on a little longer—lock up her heart and give their relationship some more time until he'd come to terms with the changes in his life.

But, oh, the risk was massive...

Kari stirred, regaining consciousness. She groaned in pain, trying to swipe away the mask covering her face.

'Kari, hold still,' Andreas said. 'You've had a fall, bumped your head.'

While Clara tried to keep the casualty immobilised, someone returned with a clean towel and Andreas set aside the Ambu bag to cover the lower leg fracture, which had punctured the skin and would be prone to infection if left exposed.

The paramedics arrived with oxygen, a hard collar and back board. While Clara fitted a nasal oxygen catheter in place, Andreas explained what had happened to the paramedics. The ambulance crew fitted the neck brace and back board, and administered some painkillers. Andreas and Clara helped out by splinting Kari's fractured leg so she could be transported to hospital.

'I'm going with her in the ambulance,' Andreas said distractedly as the paramedics lifted Kari onto a stretcher.

Clara nodded, their break-up set aside for now. 'Will you call me later? Let me know how she is?'

He nodded and met her stare, the things they'd left unsaid hovering between them. His accusation from earlier reverberated in her head.

Maybe it's me you find wanting...

Clara swallowed, desperate to hold him. There was nothing lacking in him; the deficiency lay with *her.* She'd never been in love before and she was terrified to love him openly, freely, honestly because of how vulnerable she'd be.

But they weren't alone and he had enough to deal with.

As the paramedics wheeled Kari away, Clara watched Andreas leave, every part of her aching with love for him. She made her way back to the guest wing, her resolve strengthening. She would give him a little more time, perhaps until Christmas, but then she *would* walk away. She would bury her feelings, because loving him changed nothing. If she became the person making all of the sacrifices, her love would never survive. Better to be alone and heartbroken than be on the wrong side of an unequal relationship.

After all, being self-sufficient was second nature.

CHAPTER SIXTEEN

A WEEK LATER, after a night shift at the palace, Clara returned home, her plan to indulge in some well-earned self-care—a long soak in the bath, painting her fingernails and styling her hair in an elegant up-do.

Tonight was the staff Christmas party and she wanted to look her best for Andreas. They'd only managed to see each other twice since Kari's accident. Both times, he'd sneaked Clara into the palace and they'd made love as if it was the last time, and had carefully avoided any talk of breaking up. The cracks in Clara's heart had deepened each time, but Christmas was only two weeks away.

In the bathroom, Clara removed the contents of a brown paper bag from the pharmacy, a flutter of nervous anticipation in her stomach: gold nail polish, volumising hairspray…and a pregnancy test. She could no longer ignore the fact that her period was three days late when she was unfailingly regular; her breasts were sore and she was more tired than usual. She took the test and filled the bath, pouring in some scented bubble bath to take her mind off the little white plastic stick.

What would she do if it turned positive? More importantly, how would Andreas react?

She stripped off her clothes, her gaze drawn to the test, which already boasted two pink lines: positive. Her hand fell protectively to her abdomen, her heart thumping wildly. Those two pink lines changed *everything*. She was pregnant with Andreas's baby.

After her bath, she dressed in the green vintage dress she'd borrowed from Alma, fitting matching glass earrings with trembling hands. She stared at her reflection, half in awe of the woman staring back, half panic-stricken. The dress complemented her skin tone, so she appeared radiant, and there was a new strength to the set of her posture, as if she was already inhabiting her new role as a mother.

She was adamant—the baby's happiness would be paramount.

Her phone pinged with an incoming text from Andreas.

Can't wait to see you tonight.

Clara blinked back tears, refusing to ruin her mascara. Now she had bigger issues than when to walk away from the man she loved but could never have. Now she'd have to tell him about the pregnancy—tonight.

She sat on the bed and typed a reply.

Me too.

Then she deleted it and threw down her phone. That wasn't entirely true. Part of her was dreading their conversation. What would Andreas expect of her now? Would he want shared custody of their child or would he be forced constitutionally to disown the baby? After all, they weren't married.

Nauseated, Clara slipped her feet into her heels and fastened the buckles, her mind racing with the many implications. She'd have to pull back on the hours she worked as her pregnancy progressed. She'd need to take maternity leave, and then what? There was an excellent state-run crèche near Nordic Care that her colleagues talked about but would Andreas approve? Would he demand a private facility beyond Clara's budget?

And what about their child's privacy? Would simply being related to Andreas make the baby a target? How would Clara keep their child safe and keep her independence? What if, as a prince, Andreas's custodial rights to their child surpassed her own? What if he wanted to raise their child as a prince or princess without Clara? What if he made all the decisions and she was powerless?

Standing, she smoothed her palms over the silky fabric of the dress. She wouldn't allow any harm befall her child. Her mother had raised two daughters as good as alone, and Clara could do the same. She would protect this baby with her life and provide for its every need, with Andreas's input or without it.

'I'm glad you're feeling better,' Andreas said to Kari at the Christmas party. 'Thank you for the festive transformation. The hall looks magical.'

The room glittered with a thousand lights and was bedecked with two enormous Christmas trees. That Kari was there after all her hard work, albeit on crutches, her broken leg in plaster, raised his dampened spirits.

Why hadn't Clara replied to his text?

They hadn't raised the subject of ending their fling since the night of Kari's accident. The past week had passed in a busy blur. Clara had taken extra shifts at the hospital to cover staff illness and Andreas had been occupied with a state visit to Finland and with preparations for this evening's festivities. He'd even supervised the renovation of his new suite of rooms. He was determined to stamp his own mark on ruling the principality, and the first step was feeling comfortable enough to make the role his own.

His stomach twisted in recognition of how he'd decorated with Clara in mind. Foolish, given his inability to see beyond the life-changing events of the next few months. But, if he could just hold onto her and protect her a little longer until the intense media interest died down, then he could think straight.

Andreas moved on to welcome another group, glancing at Prince Henrik, who was doing the same thing on the other side of the hall. His father had insisted on being present, and for now showed good energy levels, but Andreas was determined to keep an eye on him.

The Cronstedt family couldn't exist without the hundreds of people filling the ballroom, their tireless work behind the scenes as vital as the prince's ribbon-cutting ceremonies, diplomatic speeches and weekly audiences with Varborg's Prime Minister.

Speaking of vital…was Clara there?

Discreetly, he scanned the room before asking after the palace administration manager's small children. His jaw ached from smiling, his reserves of small talk running low. He needed to see Clara, to know that he could convince her to stay his for a little while longer.

He'd just moved on from a conversation with the housekeeping team when he spied Clara talking to her fellow nurses and the prince's personal physician. Even though the other doctor was in his fifties and happily married, a white-hot shaft of jealousy pierced Andreas's chest as he watched her smile up at the man.

She looked radiant and seemed so carefree, so Clara.

When was the last time she'd smiled at him that carefree way? Was his desperation for her hurting her, crushing her sense of independence? Would he fail her if he didn't let her go soon? But every time he tried to imagine being without her he rushed the other way, clinging tighter.

With everything going on in his life, they seemed to have lurched from one crisis to another, the only highlights the blissful moments of intimacy they managed to snatch.

Something jolted in his chest as he watched her. Were those moments of intimacy enough? Clara deserved more. She deserved peace of mind, security and privacy. She deserved a man who was focussed only on her, a man who'd protect her and never fail her. These were all things Andreas longed to give her but, because of his position, couldn't guarantee.

At his side, Nils spoke. 'Your Highness…'

Andreas came to. He'd been staring, mesmerised by her, as he'd been from the start. Deviating from the planned route around the room, Andreas walked her way.

'I wanted to thank you all personally,' he said to the entire group, 'For taking such good care of Prince Henrik. As you can see—' he tilted his head in his father's direction '—he's feeling much restored tonight, and that's down to all of you.'

Clara hadn't yet met his eye, and he couldn't be seen to favour one staff member over any other, not when gossip had already spread since the night she'd attended Kari's accident by his side.

If it were down to him, he'd whisk her away to his new bedroom and make love to her all night until he convinced her that she wanted him, the real Andreas, more than she wanted her career, her independence and her anonymity.

At last, he allowed his gaze briefly to settle on Clara. It hurt to look at her beauty and not touch her. But, on closer inspection, she appeared pale. Was she unwell, or had she reached her decision and would soon tell him it was over?

Sensing Nils's discomfort, because Andreas was on a tight schedule to talk to at least half of the staff, he prepared to walk away, panic surging through him. Then, at the last second, she looked up, looked right at him and the party around him seemed to stutter to a stop.

He stared hard, pouring all his feelings for this woman into his eye contact so she would see how much he cared, how much he wanted her, how he wished he could be just a man she was free to care for in return, without risk.

She looked away.

Crestfallen, Andreas was spurred into action. He plastered on his smile and moved on to greet the next group, but not before he instructed Nils, 'Bring her to me at the end of the festivities—the Blue Room.'

All he had to do was make it through the party. It was going to be a very long night.

For the rest of the evening, Clara watched Andreas from afar, a sense of déjà vu chilling her to the bone. The first time they'd danced in that very hall, she'd known that he was a natural born leader. He'd been torn between the role he'd trained for and the role that was his birth right, because he lived with deep unresolved guilt over his brother's death.

But his royal status shone as people vied for his attention. He was a prince. He had it all—charisma, kindness and empathy. How could she avoid falling head over heels in love with a man like him?

Swallowing the lump in her throat, Clara paced to the window of the Blue Room, the place where she'd been instructed by Nils to meet Andreas. This was the room where they'd negotiated their fling. How fitting that this would also be the scene of the conversation to come.

Clara stared out at the illuminated balcony and beyond to the vast, snow-capped mountain range that separated Varborg from the rest of Scandinavia. It was a stunning night. Crisp, cloudless skies were an inky blank canvas for the multitude of stars.

Clara's vision blurred, fear a metallic taste in her mouth. How would he take her news? How would she tell him that she was carrying his baby and still hold on to her heart? How would she find the strength to walk away? Because she must, and sooner than she'd promised. Now that there was the baby's happiness and safety to consider, she needed to be stronger than ever.

Just then, the sky above the mountain tops began to dance with the magical wonder of the Aurora Borealis, or northern lights, the green light streaking the blackness. Clara watched, mesmerised. There was magic here, in Andreas's world. But the clock was about to strike midnight and she couldn't stay.

A sound in the room behind Clara drew her attention. She spun to find Andreas observing her, his face dark with repressed need.

'You look breath-taking tonight,' he said.

Clara swallowed, her pulse a painful thud in her throat.

'More so than nature's display outside, even.' His stare latched to hers, but he didn't step closer or try to touch her. 'Green suits you, *sötnos*. You should wear it more often.'

'Thank you. This dress belonged to my mother.' She glanced down at the simple silky sheath. 'I'm recycling.'

She looked up and swept her gaze over him from head to toe, the ache in her chest sharpening at his refined splendour. 'You look very regal, every inch the prince you were born to be.'

A small frown pinched his eyebrows together. 'And yet here, with you, I'm just Andreas.'

Clara nodded, her heart cracking open a little wider. Just because she'd fallen in love with him didn't mean that she could have him as her own. He needed a woman content to exist in his shadow and, while Clara might tolerate that in public for appearances' sake, it would destroy her to know that they weren't equals in their private lives—to know that she loved him desperately, but that he didn't love her.

But how could they ever be true equals? He was a prince, a ruler, and she was a penniless nobody in a borrowed dress.

'I need to tell you something,' she said, cautiously stepping closer, because even when she was ready to walk away she wanted him with terrifying desperation.

'Okay.' His frown deepened.

Clara raised her chin, resolute. 'I'm pregnant.'

His body seemed to sag with relief, excitement

in his eyes. He almost stumbled as he lurched for her, gripping her arms.

'Are you sure?' His pulse ticked furiously in his neck.

Clara nodded. 'My period was three days late so I did a test this afternoon. It was positive, but obviously it's very early days.'

She shrugged, her own joy at the news diminished, because in the deepest part of her soul she'd dared to imagine that, if she ever had a child, it would be with a man who loved her and who she could love freely in return.

But this wasn't a fairy tale. This was reality. Ahead lay confusion and doubt for the future and fear that her parental rights would be restrained because of her baby's paternity.

With his face wreathed in delight, Andreas hauled her into his arms. Clara rested her head against his crisp white shirt, against the soothing thud of his heart. She closed her eyes, dragging in the scent of him, fighting tears.

'That's wonderful news.' He pulled back, his stare swooping to her flat stomach. 'Are you feeling okay?'

She nodded numbly. 'I'm fine, Andreas. A little tired, perhaps.'

'Do you want to sit while we talk?' he asked, clearly still dazed.

Clara shook her head. 'I wanted you to know straight away, but we don't have to sort everything out right now.' She needed more time to think things through.

Doubt flashed in his sparking eyes for a split second before he rallied. 'What's there to sort out? You're carrying a Cronstedt prince or princess. I'm going to be a father.'

His awestruck grin made her vision blur. She hated being the one to burst his bubble. 'I'm glad that you're happy.' She winced and ducked her head. 'But the prince-princess thing doesn't count. We're not married. I'm just an ordinary woman.'

Andreas laughed, clutching her back to his chest. 'A hundred years ago that might have mattered, but today my heir is my heir. Besides,' he said, 'We'll *get* married.'

Clara swallowed, dread sliding through her veins. 'Just like that—you decide and I have no say or rights? Don't you think you should ask me what *I* want?'

She might as well be a brood mare.

All her greatest fears rolled in like storm clouds in the sky. *He* was the important one in this relationship. *He* had all the power. Was she meekly to agree to his sterile marriage proposal, give up her career and simply exist as a royal appendage, too lovesick to question the arrangement?

'I'm sorry.' He gripped her shoulders, peering at her with confusion. 'What *do* you want? I assumed that you'd be overjoyed by this news, but you must also be in shock.'

'I *am* happy,' Clara said, a massive part of her,

the part that loved him and ached for a ridiculous fantasy, feeling anything but. 'But…there's so much to think about. I want us to raise this child together, but we shouldn't rush this conversation. Let's take a few days to come to terms with the news and then we can discuss a way forward.'

Once her shock wore off, maybe she'd have the strength to tell him how she felt about him.

Andreas's expression darkened. 'There is only *one* way forward, Clara. I'm a Cronstedt. My child, *our* child, will one day rule Varborg. I'm sorry, but there's no getting around that.'

'I understand.' Clara shook her head, which was fuzzy with confusion, her heart sore with grief. 'But that's a separate issue. I don't want some sort of pragmatic royal marriage.'

She might have felt differently about the institution if he'd loved her, if he'd proposed in some romantic way rather than with ruthless practicality. But she'd never once envisioned being trapped in a loveless marriage, a relationship in name only, for show when the cameras were rolling or to give their child a sense of legitimacy.

'Then we'll live together,' he stated, adamant. 'Raise our child together. It's unconventional for my family, but I'll make it all right. After all, I plan on modernisation. What's more modern than co-habitation and co-parenting?'

'You're not hearing me, Andreas,' she said, her stomach twisted into knots with grief. 'I can't live like this, the way you do.'

Not if she couldn't have all of him, including his heart. The civilised, unconventional relationship he proposed would be doomed from the start. She'd be the one making all the sacrifices, without even gaining the reward of his love in return. She'd be just like her mother: loving a man who couldn't possibly care as deeply for her; forced to sacrifice her career, her independence, to put his needs first; vulnerable, her options limited because they'd made a child together, a child she would always prioritise above herself.

'I can't lose everything that I am,' she continued, trying to keep her voice even. 'My job, my independence, my autonomy.'

'You can still have those things and be with me, Clara. I'll take care of you and our child. Protect you both. Support you always. I won't let either of you down.' He frowned, disbelief entering his eyes. 'Unless it's *me* you don't want…'

His voice was flat, but there was a question in the last word, a question that split Clara's heart in two. She held her hand over her mouth to hold in a sob. She wanted him so badly she was crushed by the weight of her desire. But this was no longer about what *she* wanted. It was time to be realistic. To set aside this fantasy and focus on making a secure life for their child, who would never have to grow up too quickly, the way they'd both had to.

'You once said that we don't always get what we want,' she whispered, wishing she believed in dreams, wishing she could escape into his magical world, wishing he could love her as deeply as she loved him. 'That sometimes we must be something others need us to be.'

He frowned, staring as if carved from stone.

She faltered. But she needed to be strong for all of them—herself, Andreas and the baby.

'You need to be Prince Andreas Cronstedt,' she said, sweeping her eyes over his immaculate suit, and his tie bearing the royal crest. 'You need to rule Varborg, because that's who you were born to be.'

'How two-dimensional I sound—a cardboard cut-out.' Disappointment dimmed his stare. He clenched his jaw and stood a little taller. 'And what do *you* need?'

Desperately trying to hold in her tears, to stand her ground and not reach for him, Clara exhaled a shuddering breath. 'I need to be a mother.'

He nodded once. 'And us?'

'I'm sorry,' Clara said, tears finally spilling over her eyelids to land on her cheeks. 'I'm so sorry. I can't.'

Clara fled, finally giving herself over to the body-racking sobs once she was safely ensconced in the back of a taxi and speeding into the night.

CHAPTER SEVENTEEN

THREE DAYS LATER, Andreas ducked his head as he alighted from the House of Cronstedt jet, the bitterly cold wind stinging his face. He descended the plane's metal staircase and slid into the back seat of his car beside Nils.

He'd been forced to keep his engagement, a visit to Oslo, but now that he was home, now that he'd given her as much space as he could tolerate, he wanted only one thing: Clara.

But she didn't want him.

He scowled at his reflection in the car's window. It was dark out, after eleven p.m., and his mood was as black as the landscape. Clara's dismissal and lack of faith in him the night of the Christmas party had stung worse than any pain he'd ever known. Nothing had felt right since he'd allowed her to run away, as if all the colour had leached out of the world.

He balled his hands into fists, failure choking him. His baby was smaller than a pea, but he'd already broken his word and let his child and Clara down. He'd been so wary of failing her as he'd failed Oscar that he'd said the wrong things and pushed her further away, given up too easily. Just as he hadn't fought hard enough for Oscar, he hadn't fought hard enough for Clara; hadn't told her that he loved her and begged her to stay.

And the price of those mistakes crushed him. He missed the sound of her laughter, the scent of her skin and the tiny gem twinkling in her nose, like her own personal star. He missed her passion, her massive heart and the way she made him twice the man he was alone.

The car pulled up at the palace and Andreas stalked inside. He would go for a swim, do length after length after length until he collapsed with exhaustion. Maybe then he'd know what to do, how to change her mind and fix this.

'Your Highness,' Møller said, appearing from the shadows. 'Prince Henrik requests an audience, sir.'

'Is the prince unwell, Møller?'

'No, sir.'

'Very well.'

Andreas found his father in his library, behind the great slab of a desk that had once seemed vast and intimidating to Andreas the boy. But now he saw it for what it was—just a functional piece of furniture.

'You wanted to see me, Pappa.'

Prince Henrik stood and joined Andreas near the fire, a sheaf of documents in his hand.

'Take a seat, son.'

Andreas folded himself onto an arm chair opposite his father.

'Everything is finalised.' The prince tapped the folder that contained the state funeral plans for

Prince Henrik: Operation Aurora. 'A copy for your final approval.'

Andreas nodded, taking the folder and then staring into the flames. He respected his father's wishes for the funeral. That didn't make his dying any easier to bear.

'You are an inspiration, Pappa,' he said, his voice strangled with emotion. 'I'll try to do you proud. You have my word on that.'

Especially when, despite being a doctor, he could do so little for his father now. But, when he thought of the future, Clara was always at his side. What if, without her, he would never be whole?

'I did things my way, just as you will do things yours,' the prince said, walking to his drinks cabinet and pouring two tumblers of Torv, Varborg's finest whisky. 'Varborg will be lucky to have you as its ruler.'

Startled by his father's declaration, Andreas took the offered glass. He'd always seen his father as a proud, emotionally distant but otherwise honourable man. Could Clara have been right? Had Andreas's guilt and grief over Oscar blinded him to the truth? Should he have confronted his demons and spoken to his father sooner?

The prince took a seat. 'My decisions weren't always the right ones. We are all human, after all. After your mother died, I worried that I gave you too much freedom. I missed her so terribly, and she'd made me promise I would try to give both our boys as normal an upbringing as possible. It wasn't always feasible with Oscar,' his father said, sipping his drink. 'I had to prepare him for the reality of his situation, but with you… I tried my best. And look what you've achieved.'

Prince Henrik glanced his way. 'I am incredibly proud of you, Doctor Cronstedt.'

Andreas held his breath. 'Even when it should have been Oscar sitting here with you today, discussing the succession?'

Prince Henrik frowned. 'Life doesn't work like that. There are no guarantees. We play with the hand we've been dealt.'

Andreas looked down at his hand wrapped around the crystal tumbler, his knuckles white. He was going to be a father—time to be the man his child would need. 'I want you to know that I fought with everything I had to save Oscar. I just wish I could have done more.'

The panic flared in his chest, as if he was back inside that crushed vehicle.

'Of course you did. You're a doctor,' the prince said. 'You've saved countless lives.'

Andreas faced his father. 'Except I couldn't save the most important person to me, to our family, to Varborg.'

The older man stared, a rare display of emotion shifting over his expression. 'I could have lost you both that day. I've read the official inquiry into the accident. I know what you did to try and save your brother. You were incredibly brave and fearless and determined. *No one* could have done more.'

Andreas swallowed, his throat too tight to take a sip of whisky. 'I blamed myself for a long time.'

'I'm sure, but no one else blames you,' his father said. 'You are a credit to me and to Varborg. I should have told you that before today. Time to lay Oscar to rest, perhaps, and live *your* life.'

'How...?' Andreas's voice broke.

Prince Henrik tilted his head, compassion in his eyes. 'The mark of a life well-lived is that you have far fewer regrets than blessings. I was blessed with a meaningful role, marrying the love of my life and with my two sons. What more can a man ask?'

Andreas stared ahead, wondering if it could be as simple as minimising regret. Could he honour his brother, his family, his nation, by chasing what he needed to be happy?

'Pappa,' Andreas said eventually, 'I have something to tell you. Another blessing for the tally— you're going to be a grandfather.'

Prince Henrik smiled, nodding his head sagely. 'Indeed, another blessing. Congratulations.'

Andreas's heart skipped a beat, the expectant flutter of excitement, a certainty that if he could win back Clara anything was possible. 'Don't you want to know who the mother is?' he asked, wishing he would one day be able to count as many blessings as his father.

Prince Henrik shrugged. 'Does it matter? If you've found love, that's all I care about. Because this job—and it's best to think of it that way if you can—will be so much easier if you have someone you love at your side.'

Andreas knocked back the whisky in a single swallow, pulled out his phone and checked his schedule for the next day. He had a visit to the local army barracks that he couldn't reschedule, but then he would find Clara and tell her that he loved her.

Because he *had* found love with a woman who was his equal in every way that mattered. He didn't want to spend another day without her, so he'd have to persuade her that their fears—his that he'd let her down and hers that she couldn't be independent—weren't good enough reasons for them to be apart.

Clara opened the door of her family's home, kicked off her shoes and barely made it to the sofa before she collapsed in a wretched heap of exhaustion. She should head up to the shower, peel off her creased Nordic Care uniform and hide under the spray until she'd cried out, but she couldn't seem to move.

Was it possible to feel so broken, but still have her heart beat? Was it because it beat for him, Andreas? Did it know better than her head what was right for her?

Reaching for a beautiful, hand-made crocheted throw her mother had made while recovering from her cancer treatment, Clara pulled it over herself and curled into a foetal ball. Would she ever feel warm again?

Alma appeared from the kitchen with two mugs

of hot chocolate. 'You look frozen. They say there's more snow due tonight.'

She placed the mugs on a side table, sat on the sofa and reached for Clara's foot, tugging it into her lap so she could massage Clara's aching instep.

'My first job was waitressing,' Alma said, telling the story Clara had heard before. 'I would come home from work in tears, my feet were so sore.'

'You're so strong, Mama,' Clara whispered, trying not to cry. 'What's your secret?'

Alma made a dismissive sound. 'I'm a woman. We're born strong. Look at you, for instance.'

Clara smiled, but her eyes burned with unshed tears. If only she'd been strong enough to resist Andreas. But no, she would never wish away meeting him. Falling in love had given her the most precious of gifts: her baby. *Their* baby.

'But strength comes from being yourself and being happy,' Alma continued. 'I've always taught you and Freja to unapologetically love yourselves.'

Clara sighed. 'Being happy is…complicated. And what happens if you love someone else, if their happiness feels more important than your own?'

She'd seen Alma's love for Lars, how one-sided it had been. How soul-destroying it must have felt to be so let down by him.

Alma released Clara's foot and took a good look at her daughter, understanding dawning. 'Then the key is finding someone who loves you like that in return.'

'Exactly.' Clara offered up her other foot for a rub,

bombarded by the image of Andreas's expression when she'd rejected him. 'Complicated.'

'Is this about your father?' Alma asked, working her magic on Clara's foot. 'You know he wasn't always the man he became in the end. We were crazy about each other, loved each other passionately for many years. We made two beautiful and kind daughters before we lost our way as a couple.'

Clara stilled, her heart pounding rapidly. It was hard to imagine her parents young and madly in love. 'So you don't regret loving him, despite the way it turned out in the end?'

Alma frowned. 'I know Lars let you down when he left. I wish he'd been there for you and Freja. What *I* regret is that you took on too much responsibility when I got sick,' Alma continued, peering at Clara a little too closely for comfort. 'You were barely an adult. Lars and I should have protected you better. But I'm fine now. You don't need to worry about me. You have to live your own life.'

Clara smiled sadly certain that, by leaving Andreas the night of the Christmas party when she'd been too overwhelmed to think straight, she'd walked away from her only chance to feel happy.

'I made my choices, as did Lars,' Alma Lund continued, as if sensing the depth of Clara's despair. 'I've lived with them, made more choices. That's all any of us can do. We can't hold ourselves back from love in case it fades or turns sour or dies. And you shouldn't let my choices, your father's choices, stop you from making your own. That's not the independent woman I know.'

Tears seeped from the corners of Clara's eyes and tracked into her hair at her temples. She was so sick of crying, so tired of feeling empty. She wanted to live, to feel young and vibrantly alive, the way she did with Andreas.

'I *am* in love, Mama,' she whispered. 'And I'm having his baby.'

Alma gasped, tears of joy glittering in her eyes. 'And does he love you?'

Clara shrugged, her heart a rock. 'I don't know. I couldn't tell him how I feel and he's…kind of preoccupied with important stuff.'

Alma snorted. 'Nothing is more important than love, Clara. You will soon know that when my grandbaby is born.'

Clara smiled indulgently, thinking about Andreas. Ruling Varborg *was* pretty important.

'You must tell him how you feel,' Alma said. 'You are so much stronger than me. There's nothing you can't do, including being honest with this man. If he's worthy of your love, then tell him, see where love takes you. It will be an adventure you'll never regret, even if it isn't perfect or doesn't last for ever.'

'You're right.' Clara sniffed, her tears drying up. 'I *should* tell him. He likes my outspoken streak.'

'See? I like this man already.' Alma smiled. 'Let's have him over for dinner.'

Clara laughed. She couldn't wait to see the look

on Alma's face when Prince Andreas walked through the door.

Except he was just Andreas, and if she ever met him Alma Lund would see that. But only if Clara stopped feeling sorry for herself and told him that she loved him—the *real* him.

'A grandbaby.' Alma clapped her hands excitedly and reached for her knitting bag. 'I can't believe it.'

'Are you staying up?' Clara said, shrugging off the throw and heading for the shower. 'I might head to bed. I'm exhausted.'

'You get some rest. I'll be up in a while. I just want to make a start on baby clothes.'

Clara smiled fondly as she plodded upstairs. She didn't have the heart to tell her mother that her grandbaby was going to be a prince or princess. It wouldn't make a blind bit of difference to the home knits.

As she lay in bed, she made the baby a promise. Andreas deserved to know that she loved him, that he was her first and only choice; that, for her and for their baby, he was the best man possible.

CHAPTER EIGHTEEN

THE METAL BARRIER was icy-cold. Clara clung tightly, refusing to relinquish her spot at the front of the waiting crowd. Varborg's dashing heir to the throne was a popular man. If one more onlooker screamed his name in Clara's ear, she was going to lose it.

None of these people knew the real him. They only saw the two-dimensional version, the sexy Viking who lived in a palace, whereas Clara knew his passions and his dreams. She knew the feel of his skin and the shape of his smile. She knew the rhythm of his heart and the deepest regrets of his soul.

She loved him, pure and simple, and she needed him to know.

But maybe she'd left it too late...

The doors at the front of the army barracks opened and the waiting crown roared, even before Andreas appeared. Clara held her hands over her ears, scared that the noise would somehow hurt their baby, but her eyes were glued to Andreas as he emerged.

Her legs trembled with desire. He was wearing his dress uniform, the navy-blue coat trimmed with white epaulettes making his broad shoulders appear wider, the row of medals on his chest testament to the calibre of man he was. He smiled a movie-star smile, waving at the crowd before shaking the hands of the officials lined up between the exit and his car idling a short distance away.

The people sharing Clara's section of barrier screamed his name and waved Varborg's flag, clamouring for a closer glimpse of him, perhaps a wave, a direct smile.

Clara knew exactly what they wanted because she clamoured too. Those things were just as precious to her, perhaps more so, because she loved Andreas the man, and the fans out there in the cold only admired and respected Andreas the prince.

Leaning over the barrier, she willed him to look her way. One look in his eyes and she'd know if he'd already moved on and made practical arrangements for their baby, but forgotten Clara. The woman beside her screamed his name in earnest. For a moment, it looked as if he might head straight to his car after passing along the military line-up, but then he spied a little girl holding a small posy of flowers and he approached the crowd-control barrier, stooping to share a few words with the lucky child.

Clara held her breath, tears prickling the backs of her eyes. He was going to make such a wonderful father and she hadn't given him a chance to be ecstatic about her news. She'd ruined it with her fear that he could never love her back. But loving someone didn't make a person weak, it made them strong. Love was the most powerful force in the universe. It made humans do extraordinary things, such as Andreas fighting to save the brother he loved. She didn't have to fear her love for him, she just had to embrace it and let it work its magic.

'Prince Andreas!' Clara's neighbour cried as he worked his way along the row, shaking hands, answering questions, smiling for his admirers.

Clara froze, her stare tracing every inch of him. He had shadows under his eyes, as if he hadn't slept. She wanted to hold him so badly, she hooked her feet up on the edge of the barrier and leaned closer as he approached.

Andreas reached for the hand of the woman at Clara's side, his stare flitting over the crowd behind as he tried to acknowledge as many onlookers as possible. The woman began to gush, telling him how much she admired him, how handsome he looked in his uniform, how sorry she was to hear that his father was terminal…

The noise around Clara dimmed to silence. He was close enough to touch now. If she just reached out…

He turned his head, saw her and froze. 'Clara…'

Clara blinked, her eyes hot with tears. She stared, seeing in his beautiful eyes that she still had a chance to tell him how she felt. That it wasn't too late.

Snapped from his shock at seeing her, Andreas removed his hand from Clara's persistent neighbour's grasp. He gave Nils some instructions, his eyes never leaving Clara's.

Her heart soared with excitement. She would go

to him, tell him that she loved the real him, and all his other versions, and ask him to give her another chance. Tell him that with her he would always be safe to be himself. Just then, Clara felt a weight slumping against her shoulder, sliding down, shoving her sideways.

She dragged her eyes from Andreas and watched with horror as the frantic fan next to her slid to the floor in a faint. Clara spread her arms wide, trying to push back the crowd, to stop them from trampling the poor woman to death. But it was like trying to hold back the tide with her bare hands. Trying not to panic for her own safety and that of the baby, Clara stooped at her neighbour's side and held her head to protect it from hitting the ground.

There was a rush of movement, the barrier parting, soldiers shouting, the crowd around her clearing. Andreas appeared, kneeling opposite her, his expression one of frenzied concern.

'Are you okay?' he asked, his arms spread wide to protect Clara and the fan from any stray onlookers.

Clara nodded, desperate to touch him, to kiss him and beg him to hear her out. 'She's fainted.'

Clara removed her scarf and propped it between the woman's head and the cold, hard ground. Andreas felt for a pulse and instructed one of the nearby soldiers to lift the woman's legs to return the blood back to her head. Within seconds, Nils had organised a circle of soldiers, a human barrier to stand guard around her, the casualty and Andreas.

The woman stirred, coming to. 'Prince Andreas…'

she said, sounding delirious that her rescuer was the man she'd come there to see.

'You're okay,' he said. 'You just fainted. We're going to get you some help. Just relax.'

The woman tried to sit up, sliding a hand through her hair to ensure she looked her best. Clara smiled up at him; she could relate.

'You're here,' he said to Clara, as if dazed.

Clara nodded. 'We need to finish that conversation.'

As paramedics arrived and began tending to the woman, Andreas took Clara's hand, his grip determined. 'Come with me, *sötnos*.'

He stood, helping Clara to her feet, and Nils urged them towards the car.

Hope surged in Clara's chest as she climbed into the black car with the tinted windows, her head light, as if she too might pass out.

Andreas dragged Clara into the back of the car, his adrenaline so high, his head spun.

'Tell me you're okay,' he pleaded, his hands on her shoulders, holding her distant so he could scour every inch of her for evidence of trauma.

'I'm fine.' She smiled. 'A little jealous at the effect you have on women, but apart from that, I'm good.'

Andreas crushed her in his arms, his sense of humour abandoned. He pressed his lips to her temple and breathed in the scent of her hair. 'I've never been more scared than when I saw you go down in the middle of that crowd. I almost ripped apart that barrier with my bare hands to get to you.'

He pulled back, his stare flitting over her face to make sure she was real. 'And the baby's okay?' He glanced down at her stomach, as if he had X-ray vision.

Clara rested her hand there. 'I think so.'

'Clara…' His voice broke, his face crumpling with anguish. 'I love you.'

She'd come to him. That had to mean something. Perhaps she was ready to give him another chance. He slid his hands from her shoulders to cup her face. 'I love you, and I need you, and I want you.'

Speechless, she blinked, her eyes shining with tears.

'I've tried to give you some time. But I can't take it any more. I need you to understand how deeply I've fallen in love with you and how I'll do anything, *anything*, to have you in my life.'

She gripped his wrists, and for a panicked second he thought she would tug his hands away, but she didn't. The move reminded him of their first meeting, their first kiss.

But he had to say everything he needed to say.

'I know the idea of my life is hard for you, but I'll abdicate if I have to. You don't have to give up your career. I wouldn't change a single wonderful thing about you. Or we can work together,' he rushed on. 'I want to build a dedicated rehabilitation hospital for wounded veterans. You can help me. We can build something to be proud of together—equals.'

'Andreas…' she whispered, tears spilling over her eyelids.

'We can raise our baby together,' he said, brushing the tears away with his thumbs and pressing kisses to her damp cheeks. 'We don't have to marry if it's not what you want, but I'll spend every day of my life being there for you, as you deserve. You and our child will always be my first priority. You'll always be able to rely on me.'

'Andreas, I love you too,' she said.

Andreas did a double-take, staring at her mouth in case he'd misheard.

She smiled and his heart soared with hope. 'I love you. I came today to see you, to tell you. I should have told you the night of the Christmas party.'

Still a little confused, he shook his head. 'You do?'

'Of course. I love you.' She laughed with joy. 'The real you and all your other amazing versions—doctor, ruler, prince. I've known for ages, but I just got scared. I've never been in love before. I couldn't handle how vulnerable it made me feel. But it also makes me strong. Loving you means I can face anything life might throw at us.'

She cupped his face, her fingers curling into his hair. 'I'm sorry about the things I said. How I made you feel inadequate. But my fear was about *me*, about *my* hang-ups, not about you. You're everything I want. You're not my father, you're *you*. That will always be enough for me. I choose *you*. Even if there was no baby, no throne, no palace—'

'Palaces,' he interrupted, his heart as light as a feather. But she needed to know what she was entering into.

'Palaces,' she continued, completely unfazed, 'I would still choose you. Because I know *you*. You're a man of passion and integrity. Varborg is lucky to have you. *I* would be lucky to have you.'

Andreas dragged her close and kissed her. Joy spread through his body as their lips met, melded together then parted.

'Clara,' he said, pulling back to stare into her beautiful eyes, eyes that shone with love for him. 'I want you to know that you can trust me. I won't hurt you. I'll love you and respect you and cherish you every day. Even if our relationship fails for some reason—and I'll devote my life to ensuring that it doesn't—I'll still love you, still respect you, still take care of you.'

She laughed, pressed her lips to his, pushed him back against the seat and sat astride his lap. 'No, *I'll* take care of *you*.'

Andreas grinned up at her, his hands gripping her hips. 'We can settle the details later, *sötnos*. All that matters to me is that you're mine.'

She nodded, her stare bright with resolve, with her signature passion, with love. This time when they kissed Andreas held onto her for all he was worth. He would never stifle or try to change this incredible woman. He would worship her, subtly care for her behind her back and love her.

'Where are we going?' she asked, pulling back from their kiss to glance out of the window.

Andreas unbuttoned her coat and slid his hands inside her jumper. He needed the feel of her soft skin under his palms, telling him she was real, she was *his*.

'Bed, I hope,' he said, tugging her mouth back to his. 'Or, if you prefer, my giant bath tub, or wherever you fancy… As long as I'm inside you, I don't care.'

She pressed kisses down the side of his neck while her fingers tackled the metal buttons of his uniform coat. 'In that case, I have a request—a negotiation, even.'

He grinned, loving the way this conversation was going. 'I'm all yours, *sötnos*.'

Andreas lay back against the seat and spread his thighs under her backside, shunting their hips closer so the heat between her legs burned through his trousers where he was hard for her.

'Can we go to the cabin?' She loosened his tie, using it to pull his mouth closer. 'I thought we could try out those fur pelts before the fire in true Viking style.'

Andreas closed his eyes as her lips caressed his earlobe, overcome with the passion and love for his sweet nose, his *sötnos*, his equal in every way.

His hand reached for the intercom to speak to the driver behind the tinted-glass partition. 'The hunting lodge, please, Tor. And call the housekeeper.' His speech was slurred with desire as Clara rocked her hips against his. 'Have him light the fires. Tell him I'm bringing my princess.'

'Yes, Your Royal Highness,' Tor said.

Clara took off his tie, her expression approving and serious with concentration as she exposed his chest and pressed her lips to his skin.

He pressed the button again. 'And, Tor?' he mumbled, dragging his lips free of Clara's wild kisses while he popped the clasp of her bra with his other hand. 'Put your foot down.'

EPILOGUE

Five months later...

CLARA LAZILY CURLED her toes into the padded seat of the sun lounger as desire, thick and drugging, pooled in her belly. From under the wide brim of her sun hat, she watched with almost fanatical concentration as Andreas swam lengths of the pool at Varborg's summer palace near the capital.

Her husband's lean and powerful body barely caused a ripple on the azure blue surface as his muscular arms sliced through the water, his back flexing and clenching with every stroke.

What was it about him and water? Clara's palms itched to get hold of him; to trace every muscle; to feel his skin and the springy golden hair of his magnificent chest; to sink her nails into those broad shoulders of his, while she cried out his name with the passion that was never far away when they were together.

Or when they were apart, come to think of it. Desperate to have him finish his swim and pay her some much-needed attention, Clara forced herself to look away from Europe's hottest, but no longer most eligible, prince. Just because she loved the security of being held in those strong arms didn't mean it was seemly to drool.

After all, she was a princess. They'd married in a small private ceremony on Christmas Eve, with only Prince Henrik, Alma and Freja as guests.

Now what had she been doing before she'd become so thoroughly distracted...?

Clara glanced at the paperwork on her lap, closing the folder and setting it aside. Building work was well under way on their veterans' rehabilitation centre, which was due to open in three months' time. With any luck, Clara would make the opening ceremony, having safely delivered their baby. But there were other projects in the pipeline: a grief counselling centre; a charity hospital in honour of Oscar; a state-of-the-art hospice facility in memory of Prince Henrik, who'd sadly lost his battle with cancer just after Christmas. Clara and Andreas had found endless ways to use their medical training to help others. That they could continue to work alongside each other was the icing on the cake.

Clara heard a splash. Andreas finished his swim and hauled his golden, tanned, athletic body from the pool using his considerable upper-body strength, all those gorgeous muscles she now knew by heart rippling.

Pretending to be asleep under her sunglasses, Clara watched him shuck off his swimming trunks, attach his prosthesis and wrap a towel around his hips, concealing his magnificent manhood from her greedy gaze.

Her core clenched as he carelessly slicked back his hair from his handsome face. She lay frozen so she could enjoy the hungry look on his face as he glanced her way. Mesmerised by his wild, Viking beauty, she watched him skirt the pool and walk her way. The water droplets on his chest glistened in the sunlight.

The molten heat between Clara's legs built to an inferno as he paced closer.

'I know you're awake, *sötnos*. I felt you watching me.'

He paused beside her lounger and looked down at her with predatory intent, his stare raking every part of her bikini-clad body, pausing at her breasts—which were almost spilling free of the tiny bikini top—the mound of her pregnant belly and lower, to where a triangle of fabric was all that concealed how much she wanted him.

But of course he knew. They were constantly wild for each other. Clara scraped her teeth over her bottom lip, her eyes tracing one particular droplet of water that slid down his bronzed chest and the ladder of his abs into the gold-tinged trail of hair that began below his navel.

'Can I help it if I like you all wet?' She sighed with longing.

Before he could answer, she swung her legs over the side of the lounger and stood before him, her fingertip tracing another droplet intent on a similar path.

Quick as lightning, his fingers encircled her wrist, guiding her hand lower to press against his hardness under the towel.

'Careful, *sötnos*.' His eyes blazed with arousal. 'I don't want to tire you out and we've already made love twice today.'

Clara scooped her arms around his waist and pressed her still needy body against his, her baby bump getting in the way.

'You know what they say...' She raised her face to his and melted into his strong arms as he kissed her, the passionate surges of his tongue against hers spreading flames along her every nerve. 'Third time lucky.' She pulled back, aware that his towel had slipped, and he stood naked, proud and beautiful in the sunlight.

He cupped her face, his stare full of desire, promise and love. 'I'm the lucky one,' he said, tilting up her chin to press another kiss to her lips. 'But whatever my princess wants, she shall have.'

His hands skimmed her breasts, her waist and her hips until he filled them with the cheeks of her backside, pressing her close.

Clara sighed, her heart full to bursting with love for the only man who could make her fairy-tale ending come true. 'I want *you*, Andreas. Always.'

* * * * *

If you enjoyed this story, check out these other great reads from JC Harroway

Her Secret Valentine's Baby
Phoebe's Baby Bombshell
Tempted by the Rebel Surgeon
Breaking the Single Mom's Surgeon

All available now!